GIFT

Gift

A Novel of the Upper Peninsula

by
Joseph Damrell

North Star Press of St. Cloud, Inc.

The characters in this novel are fictional. Their resemblance to actual persons, living or dead, is entirely coincidental. The locales, while based on real places, have been changed where necessary to fit the story.

Library of Congress Cataloging-in-Publication Data
Damrell, Joseph.
    Gift :   a novel of the Upper Peninsula   /   by Joseph Damrell.
    128 p. 23 cm.
    ISBN: 0-87839-071-5   : $9.95
    I. Title.
    PS3554.A497G5   1992   92-18789
813′.54—dc20   CIP

Cover Art: "Kuutamo" ("Moonlight") by Rick Kurki

Printed in the United States of America by Versa Press Inc., East Peoria, Illinois.

ISBN: 0-87839-071-5

Published by North Star Press of St. Cloud, Inc., P.O. Box 451, St. Cloud, Minnesota 56302.

Though leaves are many, the root is one:
Through all the lying days of my youth
I swayed my leaves and flowers in the sun;
Now I may wither into the truth.

Yeats

Cooperation is a very slippery concept to tie down.

Bernd Heinrich
Ravens in Winter

Prologue

A December morning in what the tourist brochures call Winter Wonderland; the locals call it the U.P. (the Upper Peninsula). A remote, partially timbered, mostly swampy area, a febrile haunch of land separating Lake Superior from Lake Michigan, Canada from the United States, and American culture from whatever it is that Yoopers—denizens of the U.P.—claim as their own. Snow blanketed the woods and fields; cars crawled carefully along narrow, white-caked roads, their exhaust suspended behind them in gray, billowing clouds. Mounds of plowed snow fortified the little town of Ewen, Michigan. Wreaths of smoke curled up from chimneys into the steely sky. Stores and houses appeared bedded down, their roofs invisible beneath fluffy white quilts. The local motel was full, the single cafe crowded. A pancake breakfast was underway at the VFW hall. A few skaters on the pond alongside Highway 28 watched some tourists unload their multi-colored snowmobiles from flat trailers: Chrome and contoured fiberglass glistening in the forty-watt sun.

Out in the woods, the boughs of freshly cut red pine hiding him, the old Finn sat in his deer blind watching the trail. He had seen two does foraging downstream on the Ontonagon and waited for them to come closer, giving him a clean shot. The hunting season had ended several weeks before, but he needed the meat and never had paid much attention to game laws. He scarcely breathed. The scoped .243 sat across his knees, safety off. As the two deer moved into range, heads down, stopping occasionally to paw at the snow, the old Finn lifted the rifle to his shoulder and fit his cheek to the stock. The head of the lead doe appeared at the edge of the meadow. The old man was ready . . . just a few more steps.

Suddenly, both deer snapped to attention, looked behind them, and then, in a split second, gathered themselves into coils and bounded for the brush. Gone. As if they were never there to begin with.

"*Saatana* . . .," the old Finn cursed. He lowered the rifle and, with a free hand, pushed back the hood of his parka. Listening intently, his eyes fixed on the trail, he finally heard what had frightened the deer. Through the woods, tangled in echoes, he heard the maddening buzz of a swarm of metallic locusts—snowmobiles!

The old man rubbed his chin and listened as the machines drew nearer to his blind. He pulled the hood of his parka back up over his head and peered intently out of the comfortable cave of fur and down. Then he lifted the rifle and fixed the crosshairs at the spot just down the trail where anything coming from the north must eventually appear. He drew in a deep breath and waited, his body relaxed, his jaw set.

1

Around ten o'clock in the morning, Gus came into the kitchen and caught me dozing at the table. The fire had gone out in the furnace during the night, and I had awakened at six to relight it. At dawn the chickadees came to lay siege to a string bag of suet hung on a feeder outside the kitchen window. I watched them as the house slowly warmed up, sipping coffee. I must have fallen asleep.

"Wake up!" Gus growled. He was bundled up in his parka and had snow caked on his wool pants up to the knees. He handed me his rifle. I could smell the burned cordite, indicating that it had been recently fired. "Take it down and put it in the usual place."

I did as I was told, carefully slipping the scope off and removing the stock, then putting the separate pieces in a blanket into which pockets had been sewn. This I rolled up and put into a canvas pouch. A half-mile from the house was a small clearing where an old washing machine stood. This was where I stashed Gus' rifle whenever he wanted it out of the house, which was whenever he expected to be visited by either the sheriff, the game wardens from the Michigan Department of Natural Resources, or, sometimes, by two fellows from the U.S. Fish and Wildlife Service.

When I got back to the house, Gus had his packsack in hand and told me to shovel out the truck and take him to town. I looked at the packsack and asked him where he was going.

"I have to get a few groceries," he snapped.

We drove the five miles to town without speaking to one another. The new-fallen snow was wet, so the road was fairly slippery. I took it in second gear, and Gus was irritated with me for driving so slowly.

"Harry, you drive like a farmer. Hurry up!"

"Where's the hurry?" I asked, smiling a little. I was not above bugging him from time to time. It was just deserts, considering what he usually put me through.

"Just drive," he said. He seemed pretty agitated, and not just by me. What was going on? Not that I really cared to know; although, if I knew what it was, perhaps I could steer clear, though there was seldom much chance of that. When we were a block from the IGA, he wanted out. I stopped the truck, and he crossed the street, heading around the back of the grocery store. I watched him, and he turned around. I rolled down the window, and he whispered at me fiercely through a cupped hand. "Pick me up at the bank in ten minutes." Then he turned and disappeared between a dumpster and a snow-covered pile of plastic milk crates.

I didn't mind. I was used to Gus, who was basically a troublemaker. He was my dad's older brother who had never left the farm near Ewen, where he had grown up. From time to time he'd take a trip to Alaska, Canada or Florida, but he remained more or less a territorial sort, always around—unless he was in jail, that is. Gus had done a lot of time in thirty, sixty and ninety-day stretches over the years; plus he had been through a succession of de-tox and rehab programs besides—these aimed at getting him off the booze and into training for some kind of vocation other than poaching. But only God knows what that might be.

Selling dynamite maybe.

Anyway, despite all this social programming, Gus remained an unregenerate, full-time woodsrat who lived off the land and by his own rules. At least he wasn't too greedy: His needs were, for the most part, simple; this inevitably put him on a collision course with so-called civil society just the same. He was a weird combination of hermit and town character whom everyone loved—unless he was around. He hung out in the woods most of the time, but everyone knew him and didn't consider him to be much of a threat, really. The last few years he had been with me on the farm. He had a lot of friends, but he had recently spent most of his time with two Indian guys with whom he'd disappear for days on end. I'd say he was generous with the venison, the bear roasts, the walleye fillets, and even, from time to time, his furs. The law was the problem.

The cops regarded Gus as a nuisance or, at worst, a minor criminal. His knowledge of the woods was almost legendary in a land filled with knowledgeable woodsmen, but, then again, he was something of a certified public enemy, the last of a breed of poachers tolerated at one time but who had become an anathema in these times of scientifically regulated outdoor recreation and ranch-raised wildlife. Room no longer existed for a guy who regarded nature as his private cornucopia. Gus had been busted a hundred times at least—for poaching fur, fish, game and timber, not to mention for selling the outhouses, fireplace grills and picnic tables he pinched from roadside rest stops and campgrounds. Tourist coolers had supplied us over the years with many a meal too, but, so far, he had eluded capture on this one.

I let the truck idle a while with the heater going until it got too warm inside. The snowplow was scraping the street in front of the bank, and I waved at the driver, who ignored me. By and by he pulled alongside the truck and leaned out the window of the cab. I rolled down the truck window. "How's she going, hey, Harry," he called.

"Not too bad," I answered. One never said good, as the availability thereof was in short supply and one didn't want to get caught with an unequal portion and make people envious.

"What's Gus up to? I saw him go into the back door of the IGA." Nobody up here missed much.

I just shrugged and smiled. The plow operator laughed and waved, then settled back inside the cab, put the big yellow machine in gear and rumbled out onto the street.

At an early age Gus had shown a singular aversion to farm work and so took to the woods, a boy's only option in the roaring twenties. Today there might be a scholarship or at least an internship for a youth with such inclinations. But in Gus' era there was only the belt, laid on with a Biblically driven hand by a hardcore, Finnish immigrant father who believed that the only way to live was by unending, back-breaking labor and who was determined to pass the legacy on to his sons. Gus frequently ran away to the lairs and camps of loggers, trappers, Indian guides and other such folk who inhabited the woods. Right off Gus was attracted to bootlegging, both by virtue of his instantaneous fondness for the product and his growing resentment of his father, whom he hoped to shame. Gus' father's abstinence was a central tenet of his wrathful self-righteousness. Prohibition provided an opportunity for this gifted youngster. He learned the trade from a couple of potlickers who sold home-brew in the area, and, by the age of twenty, Gus had displaced them and gained control of a large territory, demonstrating a precocious delinquency that flowered into a life-long career. While hiding out in the woods eluding the revenuers, his father, and assorted truant officers and game wardens, Gus learned the ways of the animals and became a full-time trapper. By the time the bottom fell out of boot-legging due to heavy competition, visits from the Feds who destroyed his stills, and his own swilling of the profits, Gus owned the twin reputations of skilled woodsman and delinquent.

During the Great Depression, Gus became a professional poacher of fur; a good market for luxury items naturally existed in times of penury. Gus' furs—wolf, lynx, fox, bear, coyote, mink and wolverine—undoubtedly graced the shoulders of some of the slinkiest molls of the era, who would have wet their silk drawers and fainted dead away into the leather seats of their

6

limos had they ever caught so much as a glimpse, let alone a whiff, of their furrier's nefarious backwoods supplier, Gus the Cuss. Most of the time he lived in various camps and cabins he built in the woods, poaching and living off the land, but sometimes doing odd jobs in various towns in the area—in addition to getting thrown out of bars and into jails from Ironwood to the Soo and back again via Iron River and Ontonagon.

Up until just a few years before, Gus was also known for his public displays of drunken depravity, which frequently occurred at specifically inopportune moments, such as when the civic-minded set from the surrounding towns were trying to convince everyone that the U.P. was on its way to becoming an important tourist destination and a good investment for developers. I recalled the Fourth of July in 1978 when Gus came staggering out of the Voyageur, a bar in Trout Creek, just as the annual parade was going by. On seeing the star of the show, one of Michigan's U.S. Senators, glide by in his new Chrysler, Gus unzipped his trousers. He wound up urinating on the shoes of one of the Senator's security men who had spotted him and rushed over to head off any trouble. Gus did ninety days that time and just barely beat an attempted assault on an elected official rap which could have landed him in the Squeaky Fromm Memorial Security Section at Leavenworth, or wherever.

Another time he took an axe and smashed out Ewen's plate glass windows—maybe ten of them in all—during a particularly vivid bout of the DTs, whereupon he was rousted off to the rubber room at the state hospital for a few weeks. When the judge found out that the shrinks there had given up trying to cure him and had promised to join him on future hunting and fishing trips, Gus was remanded to custody at the Ontonagon county jail, where he was put on a work detail cutting weeds with his fellow inmates—mostly local drunks, child molesters or ne'er-do-wells like himself. Gus liked to brag to me that he had his fellow penitents on the verge of a sit-down strike in protest of working conditions when he was miraculously turned loose and found himself on the caseload of Nora Paavola, one of several social workers in the county, with whom it was my own great good fortune to spend a little time each week when she came out to the farm to check on the old boar.

Anyway, apart from a few major incidents like these, most of the time Gus would get picked up by the cops for sleeping in the doorway of the hotel or bank or else in a dumpster somewhere in town. They'd take him to jail and sober him up enough so that they could get him before the judge. Then the real trouble would start. The court would fine him, so he'd have to go back to poaching to make the money to pay off the fine; and then he'd get busted for poaching and have to put on a hell of a drunk to drown the pain of his having lost his traps, rifle and pelts—and the whole nutty cycle would start all over again.

Nora, his social worker, thought that he should go into the nursing home. Even though he wasn't feeble or anything, he was bound to wind up in jail, and she thought the nursing home would be better. She and I discussed this option many times, and I thought that I finally had her convinced that he'd never go voluntarily, though officially she remained adamant and often brought it up.

Gus was gone God only knows where—this is big country with lots of hiding places for those who know the terrain—and against my own better judgement, I did the favor he asked of me. That same afternoon the sheriff showed up to ask if I knew where he was. There was a warrant out for him and this time it was something bad. That's all he said. I told him I hadn't seen him but they might check his cabin. Later that day, just before dark, the sheriff came back out to the farm and honked his horn. I went outside and stood by the door of his squad car. "I'm sorry to tell you this, Harry, but we think Gus is dead."

I was surprised, to say the least. "You found him?"

"Not yet. Some of the boys followed his snowshoe tracks from Barking Bear for quite a ways. You know that place he calls Coyote Ridge?"

"Uh . . . sure." The trick must have worked . . . so far.

"Those beaver ponds on the other side, between the ridge and the river . . .?"

"Yeah. What about them?"

"That's where we think he is . . . looks like he might have fallen through the ice on that big southern pond." He looked at me, and I guessed that he was weighing my response.

"Wow," I said. This was too good to be true. I never liked to admit it, but that Gus was a smart one. He knew they'd follow my tracks. He could be in Canada or half-way to Florida by now—or down on the reservation in Watersmeet with his Indian pals.

"Sorry to be the one to tell you, Harry. Search and Rescue is on their way out there now to try to recover the body."

I tried to look stunned. In a way I suppose I was but because Gus' trick had worked—unless the sheriff was playing with me. "It's okay," I said, "thanks, Tony."

He left, and I went back into the house to think about the whole business. It was about time I did, I guessed.

Sunday went by without incident, and I heard nothing, but on Monday I got a call from Tony that Search and Rescue radioed. They'd found his parka in the water but no sign of Gus. Probably he was under the ice, drowned. Tony then filled me in on a little detail. The DNR and the Feds, guided by somebody from the sheriff's department, had tracked him east of Camp Barking Bear to serve the warrant, but they had to give up when it got dark because they didn't know the country all that well. They picked up his trail again the next morning and followed it right to a hole in the ice where they believed he had gone through while trying to cross the beaver pond. Since Gus was eighty-one years old and it was so cold, they didn't think he could have saved himself in any event.

I listened as Tony Coelho told me all this. I didn't know what to say and then told him that Gus' old age didn't explain how he had outrun a posse on snowshoes for two days.

"Whatever," said Tony, "but there wasn't no tracks showing that he made it out, so he's probably still in there." He then asked me if I wanted to be there when Search and Rescue recovered the body, but I told him that I was expecting a guy to pick up a load of Christmas trees, which Gus and I grew for downstaters, so I had to stick around.

After I said that, I wondered if Tony would know it was a lie. It was already mid-December; all the trees had been shipped to market. I also knew he would think I maybe couldn't handle seeing my beloved Uncle Gus pulled out of the water like a foul-hooked herring. Of course, the real reason for my staying away was that I didn't want to have to put on an act, even though it might have been fun to watch them slowly discover that they'd been had. If they figured it out, that is. Gus was a pretty resourceful guy and self-possessed enough to pull off his own disappearance and never tell a soul.

I guessed he wanted to become a Missing/Presumed Dead person, a legal category, while not exactly common, not unknown either in the Upper Peninsula, where people sometimes wandered off into the woods never to be seen alive again. This sometimes happened to people who were old and of no use to anybody, and to people like Gus, who didn't want to wait around in a nursing home for the arrival of the Great Timber Harvester in the sky. For those for whom a senior citizen trailer court in Florida or Arizona was no option—whether out of poverty or preference—disappearing into the woods was the Michigan version of a time-honored Eskimo tradition: If you couldn't put muk-tuk on the plate, you voluntarily hit the ice floe.

Or not. Maybe some of the Yoopers who vanished literally got lost in the shuffle of change, unable to recognize or even find their way with all the old landmarks painted over or plowed under. Yet another new day had surely dawned in the north country. A sure way to tell: When your generation's everyday belongings, snapshots and souvenirs are frozen into the relics of history, or when they become the decor of banks and cafe walls and the subject of high school essays and homecoming parade floats.

Gus was just another one of those people unfortunate enough to live too long, who saw the arrival of high-tech hyper-tourism as the end of the myth of the U.P. as a wilderness—myth because it hadn't been wilderness in living memory anyway. Or maybe it was "wildness" that was at issue. There was something decidedly tamed about the region, and those old unregenerate types couldn't adjust to the leash, whether it was held by their families, or, in Gus' case, by the woods cops. Joggers, snow-mobilers, hikers, corporate deer hunters, gentleman flyfisher-men, bikers, ATVers and all the rest had driven away the woods characters of the past. (Satellite dishes are more common now than the formerly universal log sauna.) Like wizened, earth-bound ghosts, the elderly woodsmen of the U.P. haunted dilap-idated farms and pole-barn health clinics, sat hunched over in the smokey corners of scruffy saloons, hung around boat docks and gas stations, and worried their relatives sick, waiting for death. But like I said, some of them wandered off instead, wheth-er in step with their historical eclipse or else in a medicated delir-ium or Alzheimer's fog. Gus hoped to be taken for one of these. In a way, I was glad that Gus wanted to take things into his own hands at the end. It was not his style nor his fate to simply wither away. I was particularly glad that he didn't have to feel useless in the interim. Thanks to him we always had plenty of fish, game, fowl—whatever—plus the poaching supplied him with a ready excuse to avoid working with me in the Christmas trees.

At dusk the Search and Rescue team, consisting of three guys, all of whom I knew, stopped at the farmhouse on their way out of the woods to say they hadn't found Gus despite mucking around in the pond all day. They looked beat and acted a little embarrassed and uncomfortable as they probably weren't that used to bearing bad news. That job normally belonged to the sheriff. At the same time, those Dudley Do-Rights had an image to maintain and were probably worried that I might bad-mouth them, so they even offered me a grudging apology for not getting their man. I had to agree with their bottom-line assessment of the situation though: It was just like Gus to disappear the way he did just ahead of a warrant; since his life was so screwed up, his death was bound to be.

I gave each of them a beer and a shot of brandy, as this was a good tonic for the half-frozen. When they had warmed up some, I sent them on their way. As they were leaving, the head of the squad, Pete Saavala, looked longingly and wistfully at a few fresh-cut Christmas trees I had by the garage, but he didn't ask for one for the first time in years. Had they found Gus, I'm sure he would have expected me to give him a twenty-foot silver spruce. Very few people around there expected to pay for something as common as a Christmas tree. And rather than cut their own, they came to me for a handout, even though they had to know that Christmas trees were my only income. I supposed they thought I made a fortune off the poor city folk, but the lot dealers made the money, them and the wholesaler, not us poor tree farmers.

"Remind me to write my congressman," Gus would say whenever I complained about anything. Gus and I never had a tree. Usually we gave a few away to schools or whatever, but we never put one up ourselves. It might remind us that one hadn't sold. As far as I could see there was no contradiction whatsoever in our not celebrating Christmas. Nobody ever asked a logger to put a popple in his living room, much less decorate it. We were loggers too, only of a miniature forest. What we gave away went either to the deserving or the needy, something I felt good about doing. The rest we gave away anyway—to the wholesalers who controlled the market, and though that couldn't be helped, there wasn't any use in fretting about it.

2

A little while after Search and Rescue left, I saw headlights coming down the driveway and had a feeling it might be Nora Paavola. Wahoo! But I had been sitting around in my long johns, so I put on a pair of pants and a blue wool work-shirt and went out to meet her. I waved when I saw her, and she waved back. I directed her where to park in the yard because it was easy to get stuck when there was snow. Only December, and we already had had a record sixty inches. Plus it was iron-boot cold; the temperature hadn't risen above five degrees for a week, and at night it was between fifteen and twenty below. I wasn't one of those thermometer watchers, though, having learned from Gus long before that it was best not to think about it: The weather was either always terrible or just on one side or the other of plain bad. It was cold and stormy—February weath-er—even before the first day of winter, and Gus had gone off into the woods to hide.

Nora wore a heavy red coat and knitted black mittens. She expertly maneuvered her black Ford Bronco through the deep ruts and scarred mounds left behind by the snowplow. I made a few unnecessary gestures at her just to tease her a little, but, through the windshield, I could see that she looked pretty glum, which was uncharacteristic. Usually she was a perky, fun-loving type. For a moment I wondered what it could be until I remembered that her client, Gus, was supposedly at the bottom of a beaver pond. On seeing her, I had forgotten all about Gus, which goes to show how easily she distracted me. In fact, I was pretty well knocked out by her, though I didn't think the feeling was mutual, nor did I have reason to believe that it ever would be, occasional "chemistry" aside. I saw a lot of her because Gus was one of her on-going problem cases down at the county welfare. While his disappearance would lighten her work load somewhat, I suppose she did feel something for him. If he stayed gone, she probably wouldn't come over any more unless I found some way to get on the dole. Perhaps I could fake a nervous breakdown. Or maybe I wouldn't have to fake it if I didn't get to see her any more.

She managed a forced smile when I indicated that she should turn around and face the Bronco out toward the road. Normally she would have given me the finger, as she was fiercely independent, totally competent, self-sufficient, personally empowered and a whole lot of other independent-minded stuff to which the feminist New Agers of the north country subscribed. Be still my Tarot Deck.

Nora accompanied me into the house. I took her coat and hung it next to the kitchen stove so it would be warm when she put it on again. Of course, I entertained the foolish hope that she would spend the night, or maybe stay for good, by which I meant maybe noon the next day. Though I wanted her madly, I couldn't imagine being married or anything like that. The thought that maybe we could ease into a relationship over the years never fully erased my desire for something more immediate. In any case, nothing was likely to happen since I had had the hots for her for a long time, and my fantasy never had threatened to become real. Why should she marry a gorilla when she could visit the zoo and not have to get chased by one? All I had managed

14

up to then were a few platonic north country hugs, which, far from even remotely satisfying my desire, added fuel to the proverbial fire. For days after each hug I would remember her body next to mine, her fragrance in my nostrils. I got Jell-O knees, and my mouth dried out whenever I thought of her, a condition that, in her presence, turned me into a basket case. At least she found that funny. "Down boy," Gus would say whenever he saw my eyes glaze over, "you'll snap your pucker string."

"Well, Harry," Nora said, sadness creeping into her voice. She sat down at the kitchen table in her normal place from where she could face me directly but still keep her distance—always acting the professional. "I heard . . . and I'm, I'm sorry." She cocked her head and smiled slightly, looking at me with dark eyes edged with tears. She wore a touch of mascara and was able to sponge away the tears with a fingertip without smudging it.

"Thanks," I said, trying to look somber. It wasn't that hard, considering the futility of my dream to be with her.

"Tony Coelho told me that Pete didn't think they should try to retrieve Gus', uh, his body until next spring." She twisted her hands together and took a deep breath.

She seemed uncomfortable talking about it, and I felt wicked holding onto my secret. "Spring!" I tried to make out like I was indignant. "Search and Rescue is in it for the shoulder patches." Since it wasn't paid work, a little glory was attached to it, and it was true that a certain class of female tourists went for guys who looked rugged and whose favorite line came from a TV beer ad: "It doesn't get any better than this."

"Pete Saavala is. . . ."

"A doink," I interrupted, "strictly a budget blockhead who. . . ."

". . . is not about to hurt the image of Search and Rescue by just quitting," she said, "so it's probably true that the pond ice is dangerous."

I continued the charade. "Dangerous? Detailing used cars is probably more dangerous. Besides. . . ."

"I get the idea you don't like Pete, or is it just because of Gus that . . . ?" Her voice trailed off, and she regarded me charitably, engagingly. She reached out and touched my hand, and

I froze.

"Oh, I don't know," I said, my eyes fixed on the slender hand which lay atop mine. In point of fact, Pete had once said something about Nora that made me angry; it was nothing major, just a typical, crude comment made by one testosterone case to another—elbow in the ribs, yuk-yuk, har-har. I had to walk away from him to keep from bashing in his skull—one of the first in a string of internal emotional storms that revealed to me that I was probably in love with her. Pete was sort of a playboy and always had a new woman with him when he was out somewhere. Maybe they hadn't seen the scars on his knuckles, or, on the other hand, perhaps it was the mystique of his flippers and diving gear. I wondered what I might put on for Nora. She didn't seem like the neoprene type.

"Anyway," she said, steadying the whirlpool of my reverie, "I don't think searching under pond ice would be that easy." She had a rather deep voice, maybe due to smoking. "It keeps breaking up, and since the water's not very deep, the divers would bump their heads all the time." She saw my smirk, and the slightest curl of a smile appeared at the corner of her ruby colored mouth. She looked away. "Of course, they're wondering how. . . ."

She let her voice trail off and waited for me to pick up the cue. Not me. I was a tree farmer and a third generation Finnish American, which translated into taciturn, a quality allegedly owned by the first and second generations as well—bachelor tree farmers or not. Whether it was genetic or cultural or whatever, my life style, if you could call it that, was most conducive to listening to needles form on the tamaracks in the spring. During the lull in our conversation, I put on an oven mitten and grabbed the coffee pot off the top of the woodstove. I had noticed that she looked a little tired and drawn when she came in. Whether it was out of worry and concern for Gus or from a rough day of maintaining people in poverty, I couldn't tell. In any case, a little coffee might revive her. I assumed she'd know that my serving her coffee wasn't an invitation for her to leave, a signal still widely used in Yooperland, a custom inherited from the Finns. In our so-called household, those old-time practices

16

had long since disappeared.

Nora leaned forward, took a cup from the little mug tree in the center of the table and put it in front of her. She rested her elbows on the table with her fingers entwined around the mug. Taking care not to burn her, I poured her half a cup, her usual dose. I could feel her watching me thoughtfully, even though I kept my eyes averted.

"You said you were wondering something?" I offered, trying to sound uninterested but blowing it badly.

She was used to me. "Oh, Harry, you know," she said, feigning exasperation, "haven't you wondered how Gus—Gus of all people!—how he would fall through the ice on a beaver pond?" She watched me intently while she took a slow sip, gingerly testing the coffee. I watched her blow lightly into the steaming mug with slightly parted, pursed lips. This was the closest I had been to those lips in two years. The last time I had tried to kiss her. Half-tried. It was an awkward moment, but only for me. I don't even think she knew that I had tried. Somehow her hand had gotten in the way, and I had tasted mitten instead of flesh. Perhaps the time had come to try again, I thought, but the impulse quickly passed. As if capable of reading my thoughts, she smiled slyly at me over the rim of the coffee mug. I immediately broke eye contact by getting up and putting another chunk of wood in the kitchen stove, even though the house seemed to me to be uncomfortably warm. When I sat down again, she fixed me with a rueful, penetrating stare.

Okay, I was not going to get out of talking to her about Gus, but I was not going to tell her anything either. I owed that much to Gus, didn't I? Why, I wasn't sure. What did he ever give me besides a hard time, as he sometimes said? Anyway, because Nora was his social worker—that is, one of his would-be keepers— she thought that she knew him as well as anyone, maybe even better than most. A little professional pride was at stake here after all. But I think that she realized she knew him only as much as he allowed, which was not much. Gus liked to keep people guessing, and I said as much to her. But the whole time we talked about him—and despite the fact that I didn't let on that I knew any more than the cops knew about his disappearance—I had the feeling that I wasn't being convincing enough. Nora, like Gus, could see right through me. She was getting more and more skeptical with my every statement.

"You don't really believe it yourself, do you?" she finally asked.

"That Gus drowned in the pond?" Always answer a question with a question, I had learned in college, though my stay there was short—unlike Nora who had a master's degree. Maybe with some more education to stoke my slick intelligence, I might have been a politician or something instead of a Christmas tree schlepper. Ah, the path not taken. I probably shouldn't have laughed just then.

She squinted her eyes and turned a half face to me. "You don't believe it because. . . ."

I waved my finger at her, then put it to her lips—for me an unbelievably bold gesture. I shook my head and smiled. She had a puzzled look on her face for just a second, and then she grinned. I went back to my dumb look. It was one I was pretty good at, although it didn't come as easily or as naturally as most people thought, especially Gus. Nora sipped at her coffee, set the mug down, and fished a pack of Camel filters out of her purse. She lit one, took a huge drag, exhaling through her nose like an inveterate chimney, then lay the cigarette in a groove of the clear glass ashtray I always kept on the kitchen table. It was filled with butts, half of which were hers from her last visit, the rest mine and the Search and Rescue team's. To my dismay—and simultaneous relief—I had recently started smoking a little again, thanks to Gus. Her cigarette lay burning invitingly, but she didn't touch it. I knew the feeling. She was trying to cut down but was comforted by the ritual of lighting up and by the odor of burning tobacco. "Whatever greases your skids," Gus would say.

"Well," I began all over again, "Gus has congestive heart failure . . . and . . . uh . . . he's old . . . and . . . oh, Nora, to hell with Gus. He's crazy. Who knows what he's up to, I mean . . . who knows what happened?" I was about to find out that more is less and that the facts sometimes, though not often, speak for themselves. If only I could have finished my junior year in college: Harry Haalakaa, Esquire, Attorney at Law. Hey, it could have been so, except. . . .

Nora let out a little snort of incredulity that withered me. She shook her head, cracked an upside-down smile—the trademark of the Scandinavians—and then ran her fingers through her hair. That hair! Black to the sheen of fresh coal, worn in a longish bob that curled in like lacy wings on either side of her face. Give me her face! Thin, slightly downy, expressive; a perfectly symmetrical, alabaster-colored sculpture. High cheek bones, slight dimples. Thin eyebrows. There was always a hint of rouge or blush and so little lip gloss that I was never sure if the rose color wasn't natural. Straight teeth. From the center of her face, dark eyes glittered with honesty and caring and intelligence. Or maybe just piss and vinegar.

Gus once told me that when she first showed up at the farm looking so clean, wholesome and eager to help, he thought she was one of those born-again donkeys trying to sell him a subscription to watch Jesus eat peanuts at the October Load of Logs Festival, a new western Yooper tradition where hundreds of people stood around eating bratwurst and drinking beer from plastic cups, watching log rolling in artificial ponds and urging the kids to dig for coins in piles of damp sawdust.

Gus was intrigued by Nora's whiskey voice, however, and invited her in for a drink, which she of course refused as she was on duty and had come to try to talk him into going into the nursing home. To me, too, Nora had an incongruous appearance for someone in such a suspect profession as social work, a polite name for the poverty police. She wasn't smarmy or frigid at all.

Yet, apart from her being very beautiful and even engaging, she was still pretty formal and maybe a little distant—at least around me. At first, until I got to know her better, I thought she was a very straight arrow and professional even when off duty, a distorted impression I got owing to the official reason for her visits to the farm to check on Gus. He was seldom around when she was, but she showed up every Monday and Thursday afternoon anyway. It got so that I looked forward to these encounters and eventually began to hope that she was interested in me, not Gus. Wrong! This led to my poorly timed, and poorly aimed, kiss—not to mention a thousand and one daydreams.

My hopes were buoyed and then sunk in this fashion again and again largely as a result of my own hallucinatory tendencies, I realized. By way of compensation for the longtime feeling I had of having been yanked through a knothole while she was trying to tame Gus, she and I became something like friends, but never lovers as I secretly had wished. I simply never found a seam to unravel, and thus couldn't do anything about the way I felt.

I guess it was true that I was in love with her already. Whether she knew it, I couldn't say. To be honest, I suppose she knew as much about love as I did—which was not much. She was my age or thereabouts and had never been married. I knew a few guys that she had gone out with, but she was never with anyone long enough for people to consider them a couple. I thought she might have a boyfriend at the welfare office or back in Hancock where she hailed from, but when I got up enough nerve to ask her such a proprietary question, she just laughed and said no. Whenever I ran into her in town or wherever, she usually was alone or had one of her bozo clients in tow.

Gus thought that I was a damned fool for not making my move, but digging holes for root balls and pruning trees had dulled my instincts for snuffling. Besides, Nora had put this mask on and let me know—not in so many words but just by the way she acted around me—that we had a common interest that went by the name of Gus.

Our conversation had come to an impasse. Clearly, whatever I said was a lame subterfuge. If it had been Gus' bad heart, he would have been found—or not found as the case may be—anywhere, though hitting cold water might have triggered a heart attack. We discussed the matter of his having tried to cross the pond in the first place; the ice was simply too thin, and he never would have done it. It occurred to me suddenly, and for the first time, that I might have fallen in—that sonofabitch had sent me out there to knock a hole in the ice and leave his coat behind knowing that the ice could give way. Thanks a heap!

I was really nervous about being crowded by Nora—or maybe by not being crowded by her—and she looked at me thoughtfully. Finally she sighed, picked up her cigarette, took a long drag, inhaled deeply again, and then stubbed it out. I poured her a little more coffee and some for myself this time. We sat at the table listening to the old Regulator clock letting out its characteristic forlorn squeak with every third tick or so. The only other sound besides my heart pounding was the occasional crack and pop of wood burning in the stove and the sizzle of the dregs in the coffee pot which I had returned to the heat as I liked the kick-start that boiled, day-old coffee usually gave me when I got up in the morning.

Some time passed, and Nora eventually stood up. I started to reach for her coat, but something came over me and I asked her if she would like to stay for supper.

She looked at me for what seemed like an eternity, and finally said, "Isn't it a little late to be cooking supper?"

In a flash of panic I looked at the clock and then back at her. It was almost eight. "I always eat late," I lied. The fact was that I seldom ate supper at all, preferring instead to eat during the daylight hours so as to lay the proper foundation for an evening of coffee and brandy while I puttered around and listened to the university FM station out of Marquette.

She mulled my offer over, looking serious. Then she shook her head. "Okay," she said, followed by a warm, broad smile. "Okay!" Her voice had a strange determination to it, like she had thought better of staying but decided she would go ahead and accept the invitation. The tension that was always present between us was there still, and I thought that maybe she knew how I felt about her and, over a little food and conversation, we could come to an understanding. Naturally I had expected what she would translate that into: "Back off, Harry." Maybe she wanted to get this over with. But before I could turn her acceptance into a put-down, she said, "Can I help?"

"Help?" It came out like a gulp. I hadn't yet grasped the fact that she was really staying, that it wasn't just something happening in my head. Then came the problem of what to serve her. I hadn't given this the slightest thought. Maybe Beanie-Weenies and saltines. Or some of Gus' sardines in mustard. Food of the dogs, he called it.

"What shall we cook?" she asked pleasantly. She smiled broadly, and my heart skipped a couple of beats.

I allowed the idea that she might actually be interested in me to gain a little foothold, but I told myself not to get carried away this time. "No, you sit down, and I'll cook. You'll just get in the way . . . I mean . . . the kitchen, it's so small . . . and I know . . . where everything is . . . no, I'll do it . . . just sit down."

Waving my arms, twirling around like a dervish, stuttering: I was a nervous wreck. Harry, get a grip! Plus the only thing to eat that was thawed was some fresh grouse that Gus had snared a few days earlier. He always put snares under pine bough shelters, and when the grouse sought shelter from the snows, he invariably caught a few. Would she object to poached gamebird, I wondered? Her reply was negative, but then she had never had it poached, only baked—which confusion I allowed to let stand as I couldn't see any way of straightening it out. The upshot was that I made a God-awful mess of what would have been an otherwise great-tasting meal, but she did eat what I put on the table, including a skanky-looking salad, a two-day-old green bean and bacon concoction, and some canned pears. This was Gus' favorite meal, but since I didn't expect him back, I thought, what the hell.

After supper we drank some metallic tasting sauterne and listened to the radio while sitting on the couch. We had our shoes off, and things were pleasant enough for me to think about trying to kiss her, but then Gus was mentioned on the regional news as a suspected drowning victim who was also a fugitive. We were back to square one in a trice, as they say. She didn't believe he would have been so stupid. She didn't believe that I believed he would have been so stupid. What did I believe? What did I believe she ought to believe when my story was unbelievable? And so on and so on in a kind of frenetic dance.

Damn! I started to get pissed off, even though I was a very

slow boil. I felt that maybe she was just playing with me. She had been alternately flirty and remote. Was she trying to get me to come on to her so she could shoot me down? Wasn't this sort of thing supposed to have been worked out in high school? God, I felt stupid!

I abruptly got up and said I was going to the outhouse. Even after we got plumbing at the farm, the outhouse was still used, and I always thought of it as a kind of refuge. I stayed there for the next twenty minutes, determined to camp there all night, or until such time that she figured out that I didn't want to talk any more and left. I didn't know how else to handle her. I didn't want to tell her that I had helped Gus, but, on the other hand, I thought she'd be at least a little sympathetic. Eventually she took the hint, and, as I was pulling up my pants, I heard the Bronco zoom out of the driveway. Was this good-bye? Had I blown it? Or was this the right thing to do to a Finn Mata Hari who was pimping for the sheriff?

The sheriff! It occurred to me then that if Nora didn't believe me—and clearly she didn't—neither would the sheriff. Although it was around midnight, I decided to call him, thinking that I should try to make Gus' disappearance look good. I hadn't done that so far, and maybe I would wind up in trouble myself. So when I got him on the line, I said that it was unthinkable that they weren't going to try again until next spring to find the body. The sheriff said I could talk to Pete Saavala, the head of Search and Rescue, but he doubted I could convince him to try again. "You know that damned Finn . . . sorry . . . but he's hard-headed, and I think he's made up his mind that they can't do anything until the thaw."

"Well, order him to do it. For Christ's sake, Tony," I whined—to me it was a convincing act. "Are you the sheriff, or what? You want the minnows and leeches eating on Gus for five months?" I was practically yelling by this time: Harry Haalakaa, outraged supercitizen.

Tony Coelho was pretty cool. In fact, he sort of chuckled at my outburst, and then in a calm voice said, "Ah, Harry, you know I can't order Pete to do it. The crew and he are volunteers n'that, and if I get him ticked, when I need him on other jobs he'll tell me to go piss up a rope."

Tony was not exactly your by-the-book ramrod lawman, which probably explained why he got re-elected all the time, the Yoopers liking their cops to be unambitious. He was competent enough to do the job, of course, and he kept an eye on things, but he wasn't aspiring to any great law-and-order pie in the sky or to political office in Lansing. People expected him to maintain that laconic, almost indifferent style so long as he kept an eye on the teenagers and handled the loggers who sometimes turned a little owly when they drank and got into axe fights.

I hung up. Mission accomplished, I thought. Pete wouldn't do anything, but Tony would tell him what I said. At least I had convinced myself with my performance. Now Gus couldn't say that I didn't just do the minimum, which he always accused me of doing. The bastard. But it wasn't entirely his fault, was it? I knew that when he asked me for that little favor, I had the opportunity to immediately run as fast as I could and not stop until I was in the next county. But I didn't, did I? I did what he asked me to do. So much for my vaunted instinct for avoiding trouble.

Just a hole in the ice is all, Gus had said. Just take this popple log he had left there and punch a man-sized hole. And push his coat under the water. And make sure his snowshoes were on backwards—a trick he had showed me long ago, which was very useful when throwing off the game warden, provided he wasn't a woodsman, which, strangely enough, most weren't. "Move slowly and lift your feet up and keep the shoe inside of the track so that there's no overlap," he had said. "The wind will obscure things so they will think . . . PLUX! . . . in I went." A one-way hike to beaver heaven, and the cops would leave him alone, and he could go see some of his cronies in Florida or Canada or whatever he had in mind. He never really had said. Like a fool, I agreed to do it. What good sense I ever managed to accumulate always ran through me like shit through a tin horn.

But it was the right thing to do, goddammit. Why was the retrospective view always so contingent, I wanted to know. What did the cops have in mind with a felony warrant anyway? Hard time in Marquette or maybe a Federal prison? Or was it a way to plea-bargain Gus into the nut hatch or the nursing home? As if any of these places could hold Gus!—this a fantasy about his former prowess. In reality he was just an old man who wouldn't obey the fish and game laws and was something of a semi-dangerous crank who endangered others, not to mention himself. Who would be the first to go: Gus or the wolf? Maybe they could put a radio collar on him and have a few graduate students follow him around his territory. Well . . . Not! You just couldn't have people thumbing their noses at the law and the new ecological attitudes. Plus his yellow skin made him look a little bilious at times, and maybe a stretch in de-tox would do him good. And what had he used that rifle for? I had been afraid to ask, not only because I thought he might have killed somebody— and that was the last thing I wanted to hear—but also because I didn't want to let on like I knew anything more than I had told them. I hoped he would get caught; I hoped he would get away; I wanted the sonofabitch to die; I wished he would come back so we could live as before.

Shit. Forget Gus. Who I really wanted was Nora.

3

Around midnight I was pretty well plowed on the remainder of the sauterne. I knew if I went to bed, I would get the "whirlies"; that happened after I had had too much to drink. I would either have to pace around the kitchen all night slugging down coffee, or else resign myself to the old head in the toilet bowl routine. The thought of that greenish, brassy wine coming back up tilted me more toward the former option, although certain biophysical, not to mention existential, factors existed that perhaps even coffee wouldn't overcome. Ah, but what the hell . . . I drank the rest of the sauterne, demonstrating a modest loss of self-control and a certain recklessness that was certainly untoward. Rather than take my chances on going to bed, I opted to stay up and count the ways Gus had ruined my life. I was caught in one of his traps just as surely as any wolf lured in with one of his malodorous baits. Only this bait smelled sweet. Nora. I conjured up the skull-numbing insight that I had for years lusted alternately for Nora in my heart and in a perhaps less noble place, but she seemed about as likely to notice me as she would a dustball under the bed. Of course this was just the alcohol leading me over the familiar territory of the self that the chronic tosspot covered time and time again in meticulous, excruciating, geographic detail. Which was why I didn't drink all that often—seriously drink I mean. I liked my depression undiluted. If I was going to be a fool, I wanted to be a complete one, not infused with booze or dope that clouded the picture. Gus was right, of course: I was not only a fool but a damned fool. It was just plain silly to want something and not try to go after it. Not so much a tragedy as a cul-de-sac. It was depressing, but what else was new? This thing with Gus made me think about how my life was just a series of dull situations, strung together by no truly meaningful, or even visible, thread. I was always on the margin rather than at the center. Imagine! Living on the edge of your own life!

This damned country anyway. I should have moved away when I had the chance fifteen years before. I went to college down in Lansing to become a wildlife biologist, a common enough dream for a U.P. kid who grew up in the woods and didn't want to work in the copper mine or the post office—about the only jobs besides teaching and social work that one could call regular. But I quit college at the start of my junior year.

Mom had died when I was in high school. She went suddenly, and Dad and I were left alone. He was dependent on her and was really lost after that, and he just kind of went out with the tide in a stone boat. When I was away at Michigan State, nobody kept him company and cooked his meals. A bad case of the blues that was to end one way or the other. Naturally Dad picked the other.

Dad had started the Christmas tree farm in the '60s after the variety store he and Mom owned in Bruce Crossing burned down. The store was no great shakes to begin with, although it was home, too. We lived upstairs in what would be called a flat if it had been located in the city. For some reason we didn't have much insurance on our personal stuff, so the fire just about wiped us out financially. With everything that survived waterlogged from the volunteer fire department's effort to save the building, the only choice we had was to move out to the old farmstead on the other side of Ewen. My Finnish immigrant grandparents had built the place when they came over to America in the 1920s. They were already dead when we—my mom, dad and I—moved out there. Gus had been using the house as a place to get drunk or to sell illegal fur and meat. I don't think it was ever very pretty. All the pictures I ever saw of it showed it to be a few knotholes and tar paper patches beyond rustic. But at least my grand-parents had kept the elements out, whereas Gus had let the house fall apart. It was in bad shape when we moved in during my sophomore year in high school.

Somewhere along the line my dad decided that his roots were a little suspect, so he worked hard to distance himself from the farm and the old country, opting instead for a sort of rural Rotarian, small enterprise, golf course, civic pride kind of life style. A lot of others in the surrounding towns were just like him. Not that they harbored serious delusions of grandeur; the kind of airs they put on seemed justified by good Lutheran, Republican, north country, white guy values. On the other hand, put a crack in this middle class pleasure dome—or in the case of my dad reduce it to rubble—and full-scale breakdown occurred that self-study courses and doses of prescription tranquilizers or mood elevators couldn't redeem. This was what happened to my father.

But what silently took place underground—Father did not show emotion and, when he did, it was as often as not anger—violently rearranged things on the surface. That same fall when the store burned down, I was in 4-H and came across a pamphlet on how they had set up Christmas tree farms in Colorado and Vermont. I didn't know at the time that this was a typical get-rich rainbow that many unsuspecting Yoopers went broke chasing. It was way up there with worm, ginger and mushroom farming, scissor sharpening and envelope stuffing, except that Christmas tree farms required a lot more sweat and capital in-vestment. Mom convinced Dad that they should try it, as it was preferable to her cleaning houses and him working at White Pine in the copper mine. Somehow they came up with the money, and things looked promising, but that Christmas Mom had a stroke. Just like that, she was dead; no warning, no nothing. She was at work in Ewen at an elderly lady's house vacuuming the carpet when she just keeled over. She was DOA at the Ontonagon County Hospital.

Dad went down rapidly after that, like he was trying to get his life over with in a hurry. Being young, I didn't recognize what was happening. To me he seemed fine, or anyway things looked all right, considering. He planted around ten thousand spruce and balsam trees over the next several years and seemed to be planning a whole new life around the business. But at the same time he was drinking. Then he started drinking heavily, and he avoided his former cronies. And it got heavier still. By the time I went to Michigan State I was worried about his getting snockered from morning to night. I stayed in Lansing to go to summer school between my sophomore and junior years, so he must have been pretty lonely.

Plus he and Gus didn't get along. In fact, they didn't speak. Gus accused my dad of turning him in to the authorities all the time, while Dad accused Gus of being an outlaw and a disgrace and of ruining the community with his drunken escapades. Who was calling whom a drunk though? Then, I think just a week after school started in my junior year, I got a letter from Dad saying he was going to join Lois, my mother, in Eternity—his exact words—but I missed the meaning of the Biblical hyperbole of the future suicide as I hadn't taken a psychology course yet. He also said that he had set up the tree farm for me as he thought I was a bit of a simpleton, even though my grades were okay thus far, but in any event I would probably never be able to go into business for myself, the alternative to which was a fate worse than death or a prison sentence to a guy like my dad who remained a dyed-in-the-wool chamber of commerce type to the end, despite the overalls and dirty fingernails.

When it happened, the tree farm was almost a going concern. There were accounts to take care of, trees to plant, prune, trim, cut, spray, package, advertise and sell, so I didn't have much time to think about my father hanging from a ceiling beam in the sauna with the belt from my mother's bathrobe—or even that it happened on her birthday, putting a soap opera spin on his death that I still don't quite get, especially since my father tended toward the pragmatic side of things. Perhaps he had been a closet reader of the tabloids he used to sell at our old variety store. In any case, there I was, an orphan at nineteen—too old for the orphanage, too young for life—and Gus took me in. Hunting and fishing took care of just about any problem there was—that and work—for there seemed no shortage of either on the farm. Following Gus, as I had done in my youth, I turned my life in the direction of the woods, though, thanks to my father, I kept one foot in the world of Christmas trees.

So I didn't mind living on the farm with Gus, if one could call it that. He got his mail there, but he was seldom around, instead staying at his various camps and cabins along his traplines in the woods. Eventually, as Gus grew older and I needed more and more help keeping the tree farm going and all, he started hanging around on a more or less regular basis. This worked out okay, I guess, but however much help he was around the place—and he could work a lot harder and longer than me when he set his mind to it—he never made up for the trouble he caused me.

He was always reading, and so fancied himself an expert on everything. Finns are known for their belief in the value of literacy, and even though Gus hadn't exactly performed like a typical Rhodes scholar before he dropped out of school, he constantly had his nose in a book, magazine or newspaper. Nor did he peruse. He studied and took sides and railed and opined. One time he read an article about metal desposits in the region and decided that we might be sitting on a literal gold mine, only he thought uranium. So he dug up the hill where the spring we got our water from was located and ruined it to the tune of twenty-five hundred dollars that I had to pay some guy to put things back together.

Gus was always a bit of a political crank, too, some Finns having a bit of the commie rebel in them. One time my second biggest tree buyer was out at the farm to finalize a deal for a thousand trees. One way or another, the subject turned to taxes, and the guy said that Reagan was the best thing that had happened to the country since sliced bread. Well, up jumped Gus. He snatched my .30-.30 off the gunrack and levered a shell into the chamber. Pointing the muzzle into the guy's nose, he told him he had one minute to get the hell off our property, or it was going to be pretty hard for him to hold his water. That man took off like a spooked deer. And was I pissed off! I thought the sheriff was going to come right over and take Gus to jail, but apparently the guy never called the sheriff. Of course, the matter of the fresh cut trees for which I had to find new buyers existed, but Gus wouldn't hear of it: The guy was a moron and deserved to be shot; a violent solution, I agreed, though in certain cases hard not to consider, but I never considered Gus to be potentially violent until then.

I guess the worst thing, though, was the sauna. We had a lot of fun with that sauna. Gus' cronies would come over, and a few of my friends too, usually on Saturday night. Of course, for a long time I didn't even feel like going in there because of what had happened with Dad. But, eventually I put that behind me, and it no longer bothered me until the two Indians with whom Gus had become friends came over and declared it haunted or some such thing. The next thing I knew the building was burning to beat all hell, the flames licking the soles of the feet of the northern sky. Gus explained that we could rebuild it, and that Dad's soul, which had been hanging around where it didn't belong, was now free to go wherever it was supposed to go. This not only "pissed me up," as Gus would say, but it was also disturbing. I had wondered about these two Indian guys anyway, and the fact that Gus was talking some pretty serious gibberish about souls and such wasn't making me feel any better about his hanging around with them. Well, to make a long story short, we went ahead and rebuilt the sauna, so I quit worrying about it. The incident (arson, to be sure) sort of blended in with the catalog of typical Gus shit. Not so bad really, though at the time I thought otherwise.

It was much harder to cope with what I really hated about living with Gus. The DNR was forever coming out to the farm to look for venison, beaver pelts, bear skins, bald eagles, snowy owls, or anything else that flew, scuffled or hopped around in the woods. Did I fail to mention whatever swims in the creeks, ponds and rivers? Walleye, northerns, trout up the gazoo—even sturgeon eggs at one time. And lest I forget—as if I ever could—I was very unhappy about the scumball buyers of all this illegal tender who would slink onto the farm at two in the morning with lights off to pick up a load of fur or frozen carcasses of this or that exotic, or common, creature. The fact that Gus always made me sit in the next room with the two-pipe shotgun on my lap while transactions took place in the kitchen practically gave me ulcers. Social security, he called it.

Following these characters aboard our ship of fools came other wiseguys—the tricky Federal undercover agents—trying to get Gus to fall for some hokey sting operation: "You have any endangered species to sell?" Jesus Christ, I mean Gus was not stupid. In fact, he was almost admirably wise. Almost. I loathed his poaching, but I was coaxed into participating, at least to the extent that I felt obligated to make sure that Gus didn't get caught, robbed or worse—which was involved enough as far as the law was concerned. My disapproval took on a certain passionate and self-righteous tone from time to time, which Gus either ignored or scoffed at. I couldn't turn him in because he was my uncle, but neither could I get over the fact that I felt that what Gus was doing was very wrong.

On the other hand, the way the Feds and the DNR guys acted made me sympathetic to Gus. Some of these guys were thuggish, perhaps even sadistic, which fed Gus' belief that they were the criminals and he was the one obeying what he liked to call the Code of the Woods. The Code held that you could take what you wanted and the devil take the hindmost. It worked for him. He was, after all, as poor as Job's turkey, or had been until we made a little money off the trees, but by that time poaching was too ingrained a habit for him to leave off. Gus felt that the woods' cops were ruining things with all the regulating and stuff that they did, a point which was moot at best; but I had to agree that what science and management had done—besides giving us factory fish to catch and domestic deer to shoot—was to turn the woods over to the paper companies and the off-road crowd. Gus was a pretty regular guy, but if anyone ever wanted to see him go nuts, tell him he owned one of those insect-like, four-wheel ATVs. He simply couldn't abide them; they had changed everything about the woods. You couldn't go anywhere, it seemed, and be free of that ferocious buzzing that sounded so much like insect swarms from hell. Gus righteously maintained that they chased away all the game; his own predation stats put the kibosh on that bit of self-serving nonsense. When I dared to argue that more game roamed the woods than ever before thanks to science and the control of hunting, fishing and trapping, he accused me of having been brainwashed. Still, he was right in one sense, though. Nobody would walk in the woods anymore: For every season there was now an ATV: Big boys' toys. (Snow-mobilers call their nerdy gizmos "sleds"; a growling, four-cycle two-wheeler that will do a hundred miles per hour is a "bike": Hey, grow up!)

Gus' antics did bring Nora Paavola into my life, however, and I acknowledged that this was an unexpected bonus, even if I suffered my fatal attraction for her in secret. Once, when drinking with Gus, I stupidly told him how I felt about Nora. He called me "Swampy" from time to time after that, the jerk. Here I was thirty-eight, never married, never been to New York or Paris, or even Disneyworld or California, and I was being tortured and teased by an old man who smelled like beaver castor when he didn't reek of whiskey. Goddamn him. I worried like the dickens that he would tell Nora. He knew I really would get mad if he did, though, so it was just another one of those things between us. What Nora didn't know wouldn't hurt her—or me.

But she probably suspected how I felt. I was always nervous around her and tongue-tied besides. Not unusual for a "con-firmed bachelor." I had been called this more than once by some of the local matrons whose queen-sized daughters were at risk of getting passed over in the marriage market—not because of sheer drayage or anything, Yoopers in general actually preferring what provides heat in the winter and shade in the summer, as the saying goes—but they were at risk because of the relative shortage of eligible males, the sheer numbers of the latter tending to get reduced in logging, mining or car accidents if the youth didn't first manage to escape into the military service or college. One might even say that I had pick of the lot, and it wasn't too bad; some of these women were good-humored, skilled survivors, though there was the risk that one would wind up with a mean one who might put a hammer to one's headlights, if not one's head, if she took a notion. All things considered, though, the Western U.P. has its pleasantries, despite its reputation as being tougher than a boiled owl, and I got lucky from time to time. I'd find myself out dancing or something and wind up the evening with a friend. Plus Gus enjoyed having people over to take a sauna, after which I'd sometimes get laid flat enough to tide me over for quite a while. I wasn't about to lead a cheer, but I was comfortable being alone, had grown comfortable, I guess, over time and just got used to it. These gals with whom I was friends kept things in perspective. We were just having fun is all. That way we kept our heads on straight about it. Who knew? Maybe I'd even marry one of them some day, though it was unlikely any of them saw marrying me as a possibility, let alone a good deal. Ineligible bachelor, maybe. Gus said I wasn't interested in anybody enough to keep them around. He was only sticking around to see me through to some sort of level where I could be halfway human. At least I was known as non-threatening, an image that bothered me at first—not that I wanted to be intimidating, but I at least wanted to register somewhere on the emotional Richter scale. I guess like everything else I got used to just sort of being there.

But forget all that. It was not the same as how I felt about Nora. Obviously. I was like a puppy and did everything but lie on my back and tremble affectionately whenever she came around. In fact, it was all I could do sometimes to keep from mounting her leg, but the fear of being humiliated by her with a rolled-up newspaper restrained me. Oh, well. Too bad. But in a way, I enjoyed my failure to win her—or my failure to even try to win her—because then I never had to face her in the real world and possibly endure daily trials which all of my married friends nostalgically referred to as a living hell. They always were telling me that I had it made because I had no fate to curse or inconvenience to put up with; that I should consider myself lucky that no woman was telling me what to do. Plus they often liked to point out that hardly any bric-a-brac cluttered things up on the farm—unlike their houses stuffed full of Disneyland mementos, K-tel kitchen aids, room group furniture and endless Rubbermaid and Tupperware products, plus dirty laundry, leaky pipes, curtains begging to be washed or rehung, clotheslines to be moved, etc., etc., etc. Didn't I think that my wool blankets were preferable to a fluffy, lace-trimmed comforter the little woman would inevitably purchase, using my credit card of course, at the Ironwood K-Mart? Hell, it didn't even occur to me to think of things that way, but to my male friends—and I couldn't help but share their outlook a little since I didn't have any other source of information to consult—their wives were an alien species who had somehow ensnared them into a life of unspeakably unnatural acts, beginning with the requirement that they change their socks and limit serious drinking to weekends. "You ought to be glad you're single, Harry," Gus would say when he caught me daydreaming about Nora, "you don't need any help being a knobhead."

I was also getting used to Gus being gone. Perhaps this was a mistake: I had started taking things for granted. On Tuesday, four days after Gus had disappeared, Tony Coelho, the sheriff, was at the door bright and early with his lummox of a deputy, Norb Hukkala, in tow. Tony was normally a neat freak, but that morning he looked as though somebody had pulled him through a knothole by his ears. He'd been up all night trying to figure out this Gus business. Norb sat next to the stove sweating and glowering while Tony paced the kitchen like a uniformed spider, spinning an accusatory web around me. We started with Gus' disappearance, about which Tony thought I was being too non-chalant.

"So you really think Gus is in that beaver pond?" he asked with a crooked smile.

"Well, I guess so. . . ." Keep it simple, Harry. I had read that most spies and criminal masterminds were caught because they talked too much.

"I see. So, you told me . . . when was the last time you saw him? Saturday was it?"

"I already told you a hundred times, Tony. Saturday, in town, at the IGA. Early."

"Mmmm. You did say that. And he was buying. . . ?"

"Rice, prunes, some bacon . . . the usual . . . some lamp oil, a box of matches . . . I don't know what all."

"Sounds like he was planning to spend a little time in the woods."

"I guess so."

"How did he seem?"

"Seem?"

"You know . . . agitated . . . frightened . . . depressed?"

"Gus? Depressed?" I looked over at Norb and smiled. Mistake. He scowled. Though he was a big wuss, he could put on a look that suggested serious violent tendencies. So I smiled at Tony instead and got the same response from him. Apparently U.P. cops weren't up on the good cop/bad cop interrogation technique. Maybe that meant that they didn't have a rubber hose with them either—but probably not.

"Gus is a drinker, isn't he? Was he drunk?" Tony let a little calculated impatience creep into his voice. Normally he was always as cool as frost, but he was letting me know that he didn't want to be wasting his time. Besides, a guy who kept getting elected had to know a little about how things worked.

"No, he had more or less quit."

"Was he drunk?"

"No," I said.

"You're sure? People go on and off the wagon, especially someone like Gus who had hit the bottle so hard." He said this a little sarcastically, and I felt the hackles go up on the back of my neck.

"I'm sure," I said. "He has quit . . . been off it mostly for a couple of years." Oops. Shouldn't have used the present tense there. Sure enough, Tony noticed it. Maybe he was a little more sophisticated than I thought.

"Mmmm. You hear what he just said, Norb?"

"Hear what?" said Norb, who hadn't been paying attention, which was normal for him, his job being strictly to make it look like the first requirement of law enforcement personnel in Ontonagon County was a size sixteen boot.

"Never mind," the sheriff said to Norb. Then he turned to me and looked me directly in the eyes. "You get along okay with him, Harry?"

"Yeah." I shrugged and tried to look away but his eyes held me.

"Cantankerous sonofabitch though, isn't he?"

"Was," I said.

"Mmmm." He nodded, looked away briefly and then stroked his chin. His eyes found mine again. "And. . . ."

"You know as well as I do what kind of guy he is . . . was." I sighed and looked down at the floor. It needed sweeping. This was getting very mental, very wearying.

"He ever piss you off?"

"Plenty of times," I answered and then regretted saying it with such conviction. I looked up, and he was smiling knowingly.

Now Norb, who was apparently no slouch when it came to detecting dramatic shifts in the interrogation of a suspect, got the drift and walked over to the other side of the kitchen and stood by the door, staring at me like some temporarily tranquilized behemoth. Was he blocking the door in case I made a run for it? This was getting crazy.

Then the sheriff said, "Harry, did Gus piss you off enough, say, to get you really. . . ."

Enough of this shit! I exploded: "Tony, you're not thinking what I'm thinking you're thinking, are you? If you. . . ."

Good ol' Tony, staying cool, interrupted me. "And what do

you think I'm thinking, Harry?" He smiled.

"That, that I drowned Gus in a beaver pond," I said, exasperated with the whole thing.

He shook his head, smiling indulgently. "If he's even in that particular beaver pond."

That did it. I jumped to my feet and pounded on the kitchen table with my fist, giving us all a start. The coffee mugs tumbled from the wooden cup tree with a clatter, breaking off one of the handles.

"Get the hell out of my house," I hollered. I could feel the blood pounding in my temples, which meant that my face was probably bright red. Tony and Norb just stared at me wide-eyed, mouths open, not moving a muscle. Norb moved off to one side, a look of worry creeping across his round face like a lunar eclipse.

"You heard me, goddammit, get out!"

I opened the kitchen door and pointed. Confused, Norb stepped outside onto the porch, all the while looking at Tony for some indication of what he should do. Tony was watching me. He stood motionless.

"Out," I yelled in his face, "coming in here accusing me of hurting that old man. . . ."

Very slowly and deliberately, Tony said with a kind of official calmness, measured in units calculated to soothe, "Harry, it's okay. You realize that I've gotta do my job. Since it just doesn't seem likely that Gus would be stupid enough to fall through the ice on that pond, I've gotta pursue the logical questions is all—wherever they may lead."

I detected a tone of sympathy, perhaps even apology. I had seen him in this role a few times before when he had dealt with Gus. He would come out with the Feds and the DNR to try to catch Gus poaching or trafficking in illegal game. The other cops hated Gus, and I sometimes thought that they might have even wanted to do him in—or at least rough him up. But Tony always kept things on the up and up, particularly when Gus out-foxed them; and he was supportive and protective of Gus when they out-foxed Gus. Gus might get out on a technicality or be released after questioning if they couldn't make a case against him. Tony wouldn't let the questioning get out of hand or let any retribution come down. In fact, it was Tony who always brought Gus home, and he'd stay around for coffee and a brandy, shooting the shit with us and laughing about the dumb bunnies in the government. He was a regular guy, even if he was a cop; and to us he seemed like our cop, as against the robocops who served some abstract master like the state or the law or whatever.

I relaxed again in the aura of Tony's calm, which seemed to radiate from him. Even Norb had regained enough presence of mind to step back inside the kitchen. Tony studied me thoughtfully, a little disappointed in me, maybe, that I had lost it.

"Look, Tony," I said, easing off the accelerator, "I've told you what I know. Gus said that there was a little trouble. He thought there'd be a warrant out and that he was going to hide out until things calmed down. That's all I know. Don't ask me any more about it. He left and he could have gone anywhere. I don't know where he is. . . ."

"And you didn't help him get away?" Tony said, incredulity rich in his voice. Of course he knew that I would have no choice but to help Gus if the old man had asked me. And of course he knew that Gus would ask.

I didn't say anything. Tony looked at me for quite a while and then said to Norb, "Norb, go outside and listen to the radio. See if there's been any accidents or anything . . . or if Gus has turned up." He had said this last bit for my benefit; clearly he didn't believe that it had happened or would.

"You want me to report back?" Norb answered slowly.

"Just go listen to the goddamn radio, Norb. I'll be along shortly."

Norb thudded out onto the back porch and down the stairs, heading toward the patrol car. Tony and I watched his laborious effort to slide himself behind the wheel and then turn on the radio. I shut the kitchen door, and Tony sat down at the table. I put another stick of kindling in the stove and then sat down as well.

"This is a bugger," he said after a moment's pause. "Man missing. Has a good reason to be with a felony warrant out for him. Law enforcement trails him and suspects he drowned. Search and Rescue comes up with his coat but no body. No good reason he'd walk onto a pond when he was being pursued, could just as easily have gone around. . . ."

"Maybe he wanted them to fall in when they followed him," I offered eagerly.

Tony just waved me off and continued spinning the web. "Only one who has seen him is his nephew who lives with the guy and kind of likes him even though he's a pain in the ass. Maybe wants him to be able to live out his time doing what he's always done. This business happens, the uncle asks for help, and the nephew takes him to the airport in Rhinelander or Iron-wood, or the bus station in Watersmeet or Eagle River. Or maybe a ride is arranged with one of the old man's cronies—or how about a guy driving a truck filled with Christmas trees. . . ." Tony smiled. "There was no truck, though. Norb has been watching the place ever since the warrant was issued. Nora Paavola know anything about this? Norb said that you and her. . . ."

"Tony, goddammit. . . ."

"Hear me out, Harry. I'm not accusing you of anything, I'm just running down a possible scenario."

"Leave Nora out of it then," I snapped.

Tony nodded. "Okay," he said. "But if she's. . . ."

"She's not! And neither am I. . . . Why don't you just come out with it, Tony? You think Gus is alive and hiding somewhere and that I know where he is. You don't have to dance around. Go ahead and accuse me of helping him get away. I don't even vote, so quit trying to impress me with your cop routine."

Tony gave me a condescending look. "Harry, let me ask you one more question, okay? Man to man." He cocked his head and frowned. He was a big guy but didn't look it, mostly because he slouched. Non-threatening really, what with his round face, wispy moustache and perpetually moist lips and eyes—but now he was bringing things into focus.

I was impressed. I nodded.

"Is Gus alive?"

"No," I answered, "I don't think so."

"What makes you think he's de . . . er . . . not alive?"

"He'd have contacted me by now if he was." There! I said it.

Tony studied my face thoughtfully. "Even with the warrant—cops looking for him?"

I shrugged. "You know he's done things for years right under your . . . right under their noses. This is just the same old, same old. . . ."

Tony chuckled. "You know what the warrant said? You don't, do you?"

I shook my head.

"You really don't?" He leaned back in the chair, raising its front legs slightly off the linoleum floor. He folded his hands behind his head and regarded me thoughtfully for a moment. "Ah," he said, "I guess not."

"Look, he doesn't tell me his business, and believe me, sometimes I'm glad. Make that most of the time. The only time I want to know what he's up to is when he's working with the Christmas trees, 'cause then I have to keep an eye on him or he'll screw something up."

"Mmmm," Tony muttered, staring off into law enforcement space.

"You still think I killed him?"

This brought him back. "Never thought that, Harry, just routine questioning."

Okay, I thought, I can buy that. "So what was the warrant for? I still don't even know what he did. All he told me was he had to lay low for a while."

"You seen his rifle?"

"Which one? He has several." I felt a bead of sweat break loose from my armpit and slide down my ribs. It gave me the chills, and I stifled an involuntary shudder. The rifle! Still out there in the old washing machine. Had they found it and were trying to catch me in a lie? Maybe I should have thrown it in the river. I wondered if my eyes were furtively darting about. Could he hear the jelly trembling in my bones?

If he was aware of my rapid dissembling, he didn't let on. He said kind of slowly, "Probably a .243, although it might be a .270."

I got up from the table and looked at the rack above the kitchen door. It had room for three rifles. Two were there. "Not here," I said.

"He has a .243?"

"Winchester, with a Leupold variable scope."

"And it's not here now?"

I opened the kitchen wardrobe where we had a few more rifles, plus cleaning kits and other stuff, stored. "Not here either, so I guess he has it."

"I hope he ditched it," Tony said. "Those Fish and Game boys wouldn't mind shooting him if he resisted, or if they could say he did. . . ."

"Shoot him! What did he do . . . allegedly do . . . for Christ's sake?" I was beginning to think that maybe Gus had killed somebody or something. At any rate their interest in him seemed to go far beyond the normal license to harass and intimidate suspected poachers, which in their view could be anybody—this giving the woods a police state flavor from time to time.

"Gus is a strange guy," Tony offered by way of preamble.

"Not really," I retorted without conviction. Gus was strange or . . . we all were. I was momentarily out to sea on the issue.

"You know that snowmobile trail that runs through the Fourteen Mile?"

Gus had cursed it roundly. It went right through his trapping territory; in fact, it wound around one of his favorite places where the Ontonagon and the Cisco ran together. To him this trail was a symbol of the disappearance of the famous Code. You simply didn't enter another's territory—even when it was not legally theirs or whatever. It just wasn't done. To put a trail in without first getting the permission of the person most interested in the area—which was the person who had uses for it—was an utter breach of all that the Code stood for. You breach the Code, the sky's the limit. You have no rights. Watch out!

"Yeah, yeah, snowmobile trail. . . ." I was getting impatient.

"Well, Gus must have been hunting or something down there when these snowmobilers came along." Tony paused, enjoying the suspense. I made a point of trying to look relaxed. If I was too eager, this might take all day. He took the hint: "Well, he wasted 'em." Tony put his hands up and simulated holding a rifle. He swept the imaginary muzzle across the horizon of the kitchen, one eye closed, the index finger of his left hand jerking upward with each shot. "Emptied a magazine. Plux, plux, plux, plux, plux, plux—and one in the chamber—plux." He smiled and folded his hands on the table.

It took me several moments before I could say a word. "He . . . he . . . shot . . . them?" I felt a great black wave rising up my spine. Tony nodded. Eagerly. He was happy to be able to tell me this. He would tell it to a lot of people.

"Are they dead?" I asked. My voice sounded like it was coming from a million miles away, carried into space by the black wave.

"Who?" said Tony, snapping upright.

"The . . . th . . . the people riding the snowmobiles."

He laughed and pounded the table. "He shot the snow-mobiles, not the snowmobilers, but you could have fooled them; they were scared shitless and one guy had a rough time of it for a while; they thought he might of even had a heart attack."

"Is he. . . ?"

"He'll be all right. So you didn't know, hey?"

"No . . . honest . . . I didn't. What happened again?"

"They were just zooming along and all of a sudden pieces of cowling and engine and whatnot started flying and they heard the boom-boom-boom of a rifle and their machines just crashed into whatever was there or one another, and the riders were running every which way. . . ."

"Anyone actually see Gus do it?"

"Somehow I knew you'd ask that question, Harry. No, no one actually saw him, but Bart Maki was up there pretty quick 'cause someone had a CB, and he was already out looking to see if Gus had any illegal traps up the Cisco; so when he got the call, he checked it out and found tracks that he says are Gus' since he's had to follow that old bobcat many's the time. Plus we got motive, too." Tony seemed to be responding to my raised eyebrows. Tracks in the snow on a snowy, windy day did not add up to much, and I knew it.

"Motive?" I said disbelieving.

"Yeah, that trail is in his territory, so if he decides to do something, it's on them not on him. Code of the Woods."

"Plus it's fairly near Camp Barking Bear," I said. I wasn't going to try to pretend that Gus shouldn't even be a suspect. But they should know they had to prove he did it.

"Yeah, that's right," said Tony, nodding—and, I hope, noting that I was being cooperative.

"Is that it? Sounds pretty shaky to me," I said. "Don't you need some more evidence?"

"Well, Judge Palmquist issued the warrant on what we had. Reads pretty harsh, too—felony destruction of property, illegal use of a firearm in the commission of a felony, reckless endangerment, plus all the other charges relating to illegally shooting off a gun in the forest, carrying a loaded firearm with no license and such. Maybe attempted murder, assault with a deadly weapon. Depends on how creative you want to get."

"Shit."

Tony ran a hand through his hair and smiled sheepishly. "I know it, but look . . . they've wanted to get his ass, and this time he has handed them the hammer and nails. If they can make an example out of him—an old man like that—it'll show how serious they are about curtailing poaching and all. Which means more funds and more personnel and more equipment and the whole nine yards."

Tony was against S.W.A.T. teams and other such window dressing that gave a police department a sort of TV look. In his voice, I could hear the contempt he had for the cop army types.

"And if he can plea-bargain them down to some misdemeanors," Tony said slowly, "well, it'll give them leverage to get him into a nursing home or the loony bin or something—in any event it'll get him out of the woods." He looked solemn. "You know Gus is a pretty good guy; it's just too bad he won't bend."

Tony left, saying to be sure and call him if Gus got in touch. I had the feeling that Tony would help in whatever way he could—short of breaking the law, that is. I thought about the charges. Could it possibly mean that Gus would face a stay in Marquette, the stone dungeon—the U.P.'s own Big House? It was hard to imagine Gus walking the yard with chiselers, murderers, dope dealers, car thieves, or slow dancing in the weight room with those really buffed dudes with serious tattoos. A warrant could be out for me next if they found out that I helped him escape, I realized. And Gus' rifle, broken down in that old washing machine, sitting out there in broad daylight. Had my tracks disappeared under the new snow? Should I try to get the rifle and dispose of it? But where would I put it?

Why did he do it? He could have simply walked away and stopped worrying about the woods. Had he snapped? There was that possibility. I had thought as much on several occasions prior to this one. But what did that mean? That he had gone mad? That he was just too angry and had to act out? On the one hand, all this was possible. On the other there was something else. I didn't want to think about it.

Why didn't he just put ashes in the snowmobile's gas tanks? Or sugar. He could have found some at Barking Bear probably. Or salt; that was even more plentiful because he used salt in preparing his pelts. But maybe that wouldn't have been a clear enough statement. This was war! But a futile sort of war, conceived in hopelessness. A last battle.

Or not. How should I know? I went outside and stood in the yard by the old apple trees and looked out at the drifted and scalloped fields that ran north and south of the farmhouse. Rows of conical trees, dabbed with snowy paint, shimmering and glittering in the neural sunlight; deer tracks in lazy, meandering lines bisecting the rows; the browns and greens of needles and stumps, of leafless popples and maples at the edge of the forest, muted, indistinct, a blur of arrested motion, resonant with the blue-white sheet of sky.

4

I finally had to face what I had done by helping Gus to escape the talons of the law. I didn't want to admit that my actions demonstrated that I was no better than Gus. But this was the hardest part: Realizing that I had thought of myself as better than he was in the first place. Where had this pretense come from? Was I harboring a kind of superior attitude, a disdainful view of the older generation? If so, I was no better than my grandfather, whose old country ways, far from being lost in his attempt to internalize the demands of his adopted country, made him stand apart all the more. To the old man, making something of yourself was the measure of the man. Since he had failed to make it into the middle class, he was to blame. He had no sense of history really, except Biblical perhaps, which made him very American and, if one held the sort of American Gothic pose, very modern after a kind of hammer and tongs fashion. In his view, he should have made it and should have gotten rich or, if not, then at least comfortable. To him the misery of the Great Depression was a simple test, easily passed. The eventual failure of dairy farming in the area—due in part to climate but mostly to the rise of corporate farming, which like corporate everything else, tended to upset the myth of individualism—was caused by the farmers being backwards, in his view, or, failing that explanation, being backsliders. In my grandpa's tunnel vision, nothing should have stood in the way of worldly success for the righteous. Grandpa believed that he had no one to blame but himself, and he always was saying things like he should have stayed in the mines, or he should have opened a store, or he should have worked harder or read the Bible more. As for Grandma, she was a mirror for him, held up to reflect whatever he became—the good wife who served her husband and, if he failed, went down with him. Duty before happiness.

For a change there was a little traffic on Haalakaa Road—normally a virtually untraveled, dead-end, unpaved ribbon of red clay running past our farm from the highway to the woods—which suggested to me that something was up. Whenever anybody came down the road it was almost a special event. I had heard something though. I didn't see any patrol cars, but I thought that maybe the Feds and the DNR were using clever undercover techniques. I imagined white-clad skiers with scoped rifles slung across their backs tunneling into the drifts between the rows of Christmas trees.

I had been expecting Nora, and around four in the afternoon I heard her knock. I yelled from the kitchen for her to come in, and when we saw each other it was a bit uncomfortable for a moment because of how we had parted the night before. Yet she seemed happy to see me, and, as usual, didn't let on that anything strange had happened, as if my disappearing and leaving her in the living room was not the least bit unusual. I apologized for having been rude.

"Forget it," she said, "I know you're upset about Gus." And then, changing the subject abruptly, she added, "Say, did you know that Norb is parked over by the Johnson place?"

"No, really?" Nobody lived there any more.

"Really. He's watching your house with a pair of binoculars." She laughed, and I found her mood infectious.

"Maybe I should go over there and ask him what in hell he thinks he's doing," I said.

"Oh, don't do that, Harry, that'd be mean. Poor Norb. He'd probably faint from embarrassment, or maybe get fired for blowing his cover."

"So you think they're still hot and bothered about Gus?" It was then that I noticed that she was carrying her briefcase. Even though she accepted my invitation and was coming straight from work, she could have left it in her Bronco. Maybe it was a prop, an official symbol to lean back on just in case something more personal didn't work out. Or maybe her coming out really was official despite my invitation and her acceptance of it. From time to time, however, it somehow seemed to me that Gus was just a pretext for her seeing me. Yeah, right. But still. . . . Wishful thinking or astute observation? How long would this go on?

She walked into the living room and put the briefcase down by one of the stereo speakers. She wore her red wool car coat again, but this time with a black sweater and slacks, nicely offset with a turquoise pendant and earrings. She put the coat on a chair, took a hair brush from one pocket and pulled it through her hair a few times. I had never seen her do anything like that before, and it struck me as a very private, very intimate thing. How did she dress in the morning? Was everything laid out beforehand, or did she just closet dive? Did she take long or short showers? Did she spend a lot of time taking care of her nails? I suppose I was staring at her.

She noticed and gave an involuntary shudder, as if to shrug off my brazen gaze. "As a matter of fact," she said, "I called the sheriff to see what was up."

"Oh? What'd he say?"

"Nothing . . . nothing at all, which was strange because normally he's . . . well, not talkative, but he's not secretive either. Usually he just says what's on his mind. But I found him, I don't know. . . ."

"Guarded?" I offered.

"Exactly. Guarded, like he was holding back something . . . or like he didn't. . . ." She paused and couldn't find the right word.

"He didn't trust you?"

She looked at me, and I saw a light flicker in her eyes. "Yes," she said nodding, "I think that's it. He didn't trust me. I wonder why not?"

"Maybe he's not sure about you."

"About me?" she laughed. "How can you say that? I'm always straight with the sheriff's department. We have to coordinate a lot between the agencies; you know, dealing with clients and all." She sat in her chair at the kitchen table, and I poured her a little coffee. She always drank out of the same mug. I was glad I had washed it. Harry Homemaker.

I poured myself a cup too, although I had drunk too much already and was a little buzzed from the caffeine. Nor had I eaten all day. She was studying me with a puzzled expression on her face. I shrugged and grinned foolishly. How quickly the tables turned.

"No, Harry, come on now . . . you think he doesn't trust me. Doesn't trust me? I can't believe it. Why not?" She was serious, but her coaxing was playful.

Oh, God. How was I going to escape this one? "Well," I sort of mumbled, "maybe he thinks you . . . you . . . er. . . ."

"I what? Harry! Tell me."

"Uh, that you, uh, have a personal, that you have, that you're involved. . . ."

"Involved?" Now she really laughed, and I was just about ready to fly around the room like a fruit bat. "You think that Tony doesn't trust me because I'm involved with Gus? Harry, where did you come up with that one?"

"Not Gus," I said frowning.

"Not Gus? Who then?" She had this disbelieving look on her face, her eyes sparkling with mirth. I was sitting there trying not to breathe, but then our eyes met, and we held on to the vision for a moment. A little smile stitched itself across my face, despite my attempt to stop it by frowning. This mixed message startled her a little, and then she blushed. "Oh. . . ."

"Yeah. Stupid, hey?"

She regarded me thoughtfully for a moment and then got up

and went into the bathroom. I sat looking at her briefcase, which I had an urge to throw into the stove. I decided instead not to be fatalistic about it. After all, what defenses can a woman properly erect? A single woman especially. I remembered how quick she had been to accept my invitation to come out to the farm. She had called shortly after Tony and Norb had left to ask about Gus. It was a thoughtful, even nice thing to do, but of course I read something more into it. Or something more vague, to be accurate.

Another connection made, another about to be broken? We had come this far several times in the past, sometimes at the farm and sometimes out in public at one of those stilted community events rural Rotarians were so fond of. But what did it ever come to? Early on when we first met, I was excited to think that a cumulative energy flowed between us—was building up even. But then I noticed that even if I was absolutely certain that something was there—that she felt something for me beyond my being the nephew of her client—nothing ever happened. Simply no follow through. So what was it going to be this time? Maybe she was just being nice, or polite, or curious. If it was curiosity, at least we could build on that. But what was the right thing to do?

Nora was still in the bathroom, and I recalled the time when I ran into her at the Ewen IGA. The too-narrow aisles of that small-town grocery store helped to create a tantalizing encounter that started with both of us getting down on our knees to put back boxes of dry soup mix that had tumbled down like a collapsing bridge when our carts collided. Very TV, and we could have offered testimonials on deodorant, breath freshener, linament, stretch pants or a host of other products. Instead, we found ourselves with armloads of boxes staring into each other's eyes unable to speak or, for the moment, move. She smiled beautifully, and I nearly had a heart attack. After that encounter, I tried to connect with her in the same way, but her eyes never locked in like they had in the store.

Then, I don't know, maybe three months later, I found myself at a wedding. Nora was there, too, looking better by far than the bride—at least to me. I noticed that a lot of people seemed to ignore her, so I went over and stood beside her, making chit-chat, although I was not very good at it. Maybe most of the people there had been clients of hers or had relatives who were at one time or another, and they figured that she knew too much about their family skeletons to ever be a comfortable, casual acquaintance again. That's one of the weird things about small towns. Ultimately the people are as apt to try to be just as distant and remote from one another as people in the city, only it's harder because the small size of the town keeps people in contact—whether or not they can stand it. It leads to tensions people can cut with a chainsaw, and sometimes that's exactly what they do. Something not too pleasant in human nature makes us avoid wanting to see how alike we really are, especially in our special, secret, idiosyncratic ways that turn out to be run-of-the-mill, common as crows.

What happened at the wedding showed me that Nora was just as weird as anyone. People were standing around in this outdoor rustic country setting—really it was a kind of highway rest stop—and they smoked cigarettes and swatted at mosquitoes while waiting for the bride and groom to show up. Nora said aloud to no one in particular, "Why does everybody look so pained?"

There were gasps and stunned looks all around, as her words rang with a querulous clarity for which rural social workers were not renowned, and though it might have seemed less off the wall if the chairman of the township had said it, he and anyone else would have known better. Was this woman out of her mind? But what was really strange was that everyone within earshot instantly turned and looked at me! Of all people. Hey, why me? What did I have to do with it? I was just as shocked at Nora's comment as everyone else.

Anyway, after a few seconds of absolute panic, I kind of whispered to her behind my hand, "Nobody's sure if Randy is really serious about Jean, or if she can take living up here."

The wedding was one of those local-yokel-marries-outsider deals. Bringing an outsider into the community required the kind of commitment that boys growing up in the western end of the

Upper Peninsula seldom made—their top priorities being hunting and fishing—and let the wife do what she wanted. This seldom took with downstate brides who often as not went back to Mom and Dad during the brief but promising February thaw.

But leave it to Nora. She replied in a loud voice, "Who's to say what's serious nowadays?" True, true, but best not talk about it.

Several people, showing their displeasure—it was as if the wedding, if not the marriage, had been jinxed—quickly moved away and left us standing alone. For about a micro-second, Nora and I had high-tension lines strung between us at a number of electrically charged terminals. We looked into each other's eyes and . . . instant communication. I nearly blew a fuse and was buzzing for days afterwards. But the next time I saw her when she came over—to check on Gus of course—she acted like nothing had happened. Perhaps nothing had. I had been hallucinating again, I decided, an occupational hazard for the working, womanless recluse, the proprietor of a Christmas tree farm.

Nora came out of the bathroom and asked if she could use the phone. While she dialed, I stepped outside to catch my breath and try to calm down. I looked out at the darkness that seemed to rise out of the trees and spread itself into the ground and sky. The farm. Now a going concern, although the designation tree farm qualified the original somewhat. No dairy cows now, nor the mean bull Grandpa had, nor the crazed, slobbering, killer dog who always nearly garrotted himself on his chain trying to maul whomever came into the yard.

When the variety store my folks owned burned down and we moved, the farm, which never had been much in the way of a business, was in a barbarous state of neglect. The barn was stove in; all that remained of the chicken house was a foundation and a jumble of splintered, shit-stained boards. But most obvious of all was the ruined, neglected land, whose fields were full of brush and were criss-crossed by veined ditches cut by years of unchecked spring run-off. Things had been going downhill for twenty years. My grandfather had injured himself on a tractor one spring in the fifties and hadn't been able to farm very energetically or keep the place up after that. Gus and my dad helped, and so did Mom, Grandma and I, but it was never enough. Dad and Gus mowed and bailed hay twice or three times a season depending on the weather, but eventually there was nothing to do with it as the dairy industry disappeared due to technological innovations and the big companies underselling everyone. The cows were either sold off or eaten, the horse team grew old and died, and the bull had to be destroyed after he tangled with a sow black bear which had ventured into the barn to eat grain with her cubs.

I hate to think about the sauna, which was a travesty. If not the heart of the Haalakaa farm, it had been the soul. The chimney was splavened, the benches broken, and the wide open roof with its sad exposed rafters had become the yawning portal for a flock of pigeons. Inside, the stove was all busted up and rusty, the floor had been gnawed away by termites, woodchucks and rats, and the windows were punched out with raggedy shreds of curtains flapping in the breeze. I couldn't bear to look at the place, and Mom finally set me to work cleaning it up that summer and after school in the fall when I was finished with my other chores. We always took our saunas Saturday nights at the Johnson's place up the road, which satisfied our need for steam communion, but that bath house of ours remained a sore point. Eventually Dad and Gus decided to do something about it, and, by late fall, we had a sauna again. Mom died that same Christmas, but at least she lived to see the preservation of a piece of family history. What she would have thought of Dad's hanging himself in there, or of Gus' burning it down, and our rebuilding it once more, I could only guess. She never was very talkative, and I could see her just shaking her head. One thing I remembered her saying, and, though I didn't remember the context, I guessed it applied kind of across the board: Men are fools, and women marry them. She found her solace in quilting, and I regretted that I didn't have a single one she made.

I went back inside to find Nora still on the phone. I watched her for a few minutes, and she sort of rolled her eyes and wiggled her fingers to indicate that whomever she had on the line sure was a talker. So I decided I had better get supper started and went down into the basement to get a few vegetables from the root cellar. The basement was a dank but inviting place that never benefitted from the work that was done on the rest of the house. When we moved out there, Dad hired a couple of hands to help us do some so-called remodeling, which in the U.P. usually meant lumberyard interior paneling, a spartan gas station-style bathroom (it was the first time the place had running water other than a hand pump), new linoleum throughout, some replacement sashes and storm doors. Outside we built a new garage, fixed the sagging back porch on the house, put on a new roof and then slapped up some cheap siding to cover up the rustic-looking but shrunken, leaky and weathered cedar log walls. A strictly Philistine approach, but these simple repairs rescued the house from the oblivion that was the fate of hundreds just like it across the U.P. Although the farm was not a farm any more in the strict sense of the term, it was once again home to our family. The thousands of Christmas trees that eventually crowded the former hay fields gave the place an entirely new identity. I suppose the fact that Gus and I were the last survivors gave it a certain flavor as well. We made some pair.

Not that we stood out in the crowd. There were lots of characters, you might say, in the area—families that had aged, lost the parents, with the kids moved away to greener pastures or subdivisions downstate, and just the skeleton crews left to hang around. Old, broken-down farm houses, some of them halfway fixed up, and a lot of new kit homes looking uniformly forlorn and out of place, not to mention the little towns with their sagging dry goods and feed stores, greasy gas stations, senior citizen centers, lonely hotels, one-room banks and libraries and smoky saloons and an occasional cafe serving sloppy joes and meat loaf, and, on Fridays—Vatican streamlining of the faith notwithstanding—fish fry.

Nora hung up the phone and came back into the kitchen and sat down. "Work, work, work," I said.

"I know it. I'm sorry," she replied.

"It's nice that you could come over."

"It's nice to be here. Thanks for inviting me. But it's kind of official too." She looked radiant, but I tried not to notice.

"I figured," I said.

"Well not really official, but my supervisor gave me papers he wants you to look at." She took them out of her briefcase and handed them to me.

I looked them over and handed them back. "What's this about?"

"The usual," she said. "It's a form for the nursing home. If Gus happened to be here, I thought maybe he could at least look at them and decide whether. . . ."

"Well, he's not here, and even if he were. . . ."

"I know, I told my supervisor that, but. . . ."

"Doesn't matter. You up for some venison?"

"That'd be great," she said.

"I'm glad you're here," I said again.

"Me too." She smiled so sweetly I thought I would die of happiness. Obviously more than casework was going on here. I put my hands in my pockets so she wouldn't see them shaking. "About last night . . . was anything wrong . . . did I say something?"

"No, I was just upset about Gus."

"Oh." She frowned, uncomfortable with my inability to say more.

Venison this time. This deer more or less legal as Gus had actually tagged it during the hunting season—although not with his own tag. I marinated some of the tenderloin in red wine and garlic and then flash fried it to seal in the juices before putting it to broil in the oven. I made up a salad and fixed a dish of mixed frozen vegetables and some wild rice. Beer with the meal; donuts and coffee for dessert. Cuisine d'Yooper, eaten largely in silence, absent the polite repartee one is required to make over more mediocre fare. I would have to say it was pretty tasty grub, and Nora seemed genuinely pleased and surprised after the poached partridge fiasco of the previous evening. A pleasant mood emerged.

After we cleared the table, we moved into the living room.

I didn't have to use a single one of my subtle playboy moves, as we seemed very much in sync for the first time. The living room was a little alien. It had an almost museum-like ambience because we seldom used it. It had gold and brown upholstered furniture with doilies on the arms, a red and white hooked rug, a mica-windowed, polished steel parlor stove and heavy red drapes. On the brightly papered walls, the sepia-toned portraits of Grandpa and family stared apostolic daggers at us from across the spiritual chasm of the generations. Nora was relaxed, despite the somber, almost funereal, formality of the room, and I even managed to sit still for a while before jumping up to do the dishes. She turned on the radio and found a jazz program on the Rhine-lander station. But it was cowboy jazz with fiddles, which always made me jumpy.

Naturally I was still unsure of myself despite the good feeling that had settled upon us. And it didn't help matters much when she started talking about Gus' disappearance again and asking me if I thought he would get in touch with me soon. I realized her questions were innocent, and I wanted to kick myself for my behavior the previous night when I stormed out of the house and left her there. How could I believe that she had been pimping for the sheriff? I looked around for her briefcase. She had put it by the door.

"You interested in Gus professionally or what?" I asked her. I regretted putting it that way, and she looked a little hurt.

"Well, I guess I understand why you'd ask," she said. "You could say it's both professional and personal."

And then I decided to tell her. I didn't care what happened. "I expect he'll be in touch, but I don't know when. He expects that things will settle down to a dull roar when the sheriff and the government guys find better things to do."

She touched my arm and smiled. Apparently she wasn't the least bit surprised by my statement. "That could be quite a long wait then. I think they really want him this time because of the rifle . . . those people were really shook up. One guy especially. So Tony's under a lot of pressure to do something."

"You think I should take Norb a cup of coffee?"

She laughed. It made sense that Tony would have to make it look good. Not that he was a piker when it came to enforcing the law, but he tended to handle things in his own way. He'd have been on Gus' case anyway and probably would have confiscated the rifle and made him pay restitution for the ruined snowmobiles, but with the Feds and the DNR involved, he might have to. . . .

I put away the last of the dishes, and we went back into the living room. I said, "Tony should just declare him missing and presumed. . . ."

She was shaking her head, so I didn't finish. Okay, so this was not going to end soon. The circumstantial evidence was probably strong enough to get him indicted. A jury trial might be a problem, however, because the locals might not want to put one of their own away even though public opinion was officially anti-poaching, while private opinion tended to side with the old timers. On the other hand, if the cops got him, they might ply him with brandy and schnapps, use a little downstate police science and trick him into confessing.

In the meantime, I was feeling light-headed from the rush of protein and justifications. Watching Nora drink wine from a juice glass was hitting me hard. I was falling in love with her all over again—a nearly daily occurrence. Her skin glowed in the light cast by the parlor stove. Her pupils were dilated; her lips slightly parted, moist, red, inviting. Somehow her hair had gotten mussed up. She took off her blue turquoise necklace and earrings and rested her head against the back of the sofa. I smiled and she laughed, a tender chuckle that was at once inviting and ironic.

At last we were completely at ease. It had taken us a long time. Such a strange biophysical ritual, facilitated by three bottles of Gallo wine which she had picked up in Bruce Crossing that afternoon and had transported to the farm in—of all things— her famous official social worker briefcase. Taking our time, savoring each step of our approach, we had some cheesecake I had made and then frozen a few weeks earlier. It was a bit heavy on top of the venison and donuts, but I was not above overstatement. After the initial sugar rush, we moved toward a langorous, sensual intimacy.

Then, finally, the beginning silence of lovers. When we finally kissed, it was a new and at the same time familiar feeling for both of us—something to be explored again and again.

She left just before seven the next morning as she had to be at work by eight. I could still taste her and held my hands up to my face to breathe in once more her waking, quick-warm smell . . . discovering on my pillow a few strands of her hair which I picked up and examined in the gathering light of false dawn.

5

Later that morning it snowed again, a thin fluffy layer added to the previous weekend's laminate of ice. A wind came up, and vibrant, translucent clouds of swirling white were thrown up from the drifts. These animated, ghostly shapes skipped over the fields with a purposeful wildness, clinging briefly to the rows of half-buried Christmas trees until, abandoning a haven among the boughs, they pounced upon the rubble of the old farm buildings, flew past the north face of the sauna's chimney, and finally tumbled across the yard and into the south forty where they gathered themselves up, forming an opaque, crystalline wall rushing to the edge of the woods, where they again broke into vaporous streams sucked into the black curtain of the forest's outer edge.

Feeling simultaneously serene and enervated, I watched all this through the kitchen window as I sat at the table drinking my morning coffee. I was further unnerved by the sudden appearance of a train of raven pairs cutting across the wind, headed east toward the river, their tarry sheen and processional flight, their rhythmic flapping and determined purpose a shocking contrast to the apparent randomness of the whiteout—and of my thoughts. I should have expected to be confused rather than fulfilled. My hands were trembling, my mouth dry despite the coffee. I felt my chest and ruled out a heart attack. My crazy wish to be with Nora had come true, but now what? Nora had abandoned herself to our lovemaking and I had . . . what? . . . reciprocated? It was hard for me to see myself as her lover. Or anyone's. It was different from the other women I had been with, as they say. I was not just a generic lay; Nora had loved me. As in Me! What was expected of me now? Should I call her? Wait until she called me? Do nothing? Was it possible that she might act as though nothing had happened? Or was everything different now? It didn't seem like it. It was the strangest thing to still have to face the same questions as before. I had thought that our making love would produce the answer.

The telephone must have been ringing a long time because I remembered hearing it, but, for some reason, it didn't occur to me to pick it up right away. Of course it was the last person I expected to hear from, although logically it was the only person who might have reason to call me—other than Ed McMahon with my ten million dollars, I mean.

"Nora. . . ."

"Harry, I just found out that one of the snowmobilers . . . you know the guy who almost had a heart attack. . . ?"

"I remember Tony saying something about. . . ."

"Well he's dead. . . ."

"Jesus."

"They all got back to the motel where they were staying, and this morning he said he wasn't feeling well again . . . and . . . I don't know exactly what happened. But by the time they got him back to the hospital in Ontonagon he was. . . ."

"Oh, God, and I'll bet they're saying that Gus. . . ."

"Exactly. I called the sheriff's office, and Tony wouldn't talk to me. You were right about him by the way. I couldn't imagine! Anyway, the dispatcher said that they've gone back to the judge with a voluntary manslaughter charge." Her voice was very controlled. I was impressed with how calm she was. Unlike me. I couldn't think: Images of Gus on the run, trailed by packs of ATV riding lawmen, their radios squawking and sirens whining, weapons in hand; of search parties smashing through the door of Barking Bear, throwing Gus to the floor, handcuffing him and hustling him back through the woods; of Gus riding in a squad car, his head lowered; of Gus booked and put in a cell; of the court dates; of the trial, and, finally, of the stony lonesome. Welcome to our world, old man, say the guys in the yard.

"Harry, Harry, are you still there? Can you hear me?" Nora's voice had an alarming ring to it now.

"Yeah, yeah, I'm sorry, I. . . ."

"I know, but you have to stay calm. Listen, there's more. Do you know Priscilla Ackley?" She said this in a near whisper, so I had to concentrate to hear her.

"Who?"

"She's a social worker on the reservation at Watersmeet and. . . ."

"I . . . I don't think I know her . . . what about. . . ?"

"Never mind . . . anyway, she came up to the office this morning and said that when she was visiting a client, a Mrs. DuPree, one of the lady's grandchildren who was in the house asked when she could go home. . . ."

"Who? Mrs. Du. . . ." I couldn't figure out what Nora was talking about.

"Harry, listen a minute." Her voice hardened as she carefully measured her words.

"Okay, sorry, go ahead." I was fighting down a rising wave of panic. I had gotten up and was pacing around the kitchen, stopping when I pulled the phone off the table. It banged on the kitchen floor, and I fumbled with it trying to pick it up. "Sorry . . . I just dropped the phone is all. . . ."

"Anyway . . . this Mrs. DuPree's granddaughter asked her how long that old white man was going to be staying, because she wanted to go back to her father's house to play Nintendo." Nora paused, patiently waiting for me to make some connection.

"Her father's . . . I don't. . . ."

"Harry . . . not her father . . . an old white man staying on the reservation. . . ."

"Reservation . . . oh . . . what? . . . I, uh." As in, Harry, you dumbhead, she's talking about Gus! Wow. "Gus?"

"Exactly. Anyway, that's what I thought, so I called around, and you know those Indian guys Gus hangs around with sometimes. . . ."

"Eddie . . . and Dan . . . what's his name?"

"Right, right, I got ahold of Eddie, and he said Gus is staying in a trailer on the end of Fish Hatchery Road, and he's ready to leave and wants you to come get him right away."

"Have you looked outside? It's snowing to beat hell. How am I supposed to. . . ."

"Harry, they're probably watching the farm. The dispatcher said they were going to bring him in no matter what because now . . . you know, the snowmobiler and all. . . ."

"Well, how am I supposed to drive over there with blowing snow everywhere?"

"The Bronco has four-wheel drive, so it'll make it. I'll take the afternoon off and come and get you."

"Okay."

But rather than risk encountering roaming cops, which would undoubtedly happen if she drove to the farm to pick me up, we decided that I should take the snowmobile north, following an old trail my grandfather had made behind the abandoned Johnson place. We would meet where the woods butted up against the old highway just west of Ewen. I could stay out of sight of Haalakaa Road the entire way.

I put on my boots, insulated coveralls, parka and cap, grabbed a pair of mittens from off the woodbox on the porch and went outside. Looking up the driveway through the gusts of blowing snow, I could make out the vague outline of a car parked up on the road. I thought that it was probably the deputy, Norb, although it could have been somebody more professional. I hustled over to the garage and went in through the side door. Inside was my old snowmobile, an almost prehistoric Ski-doo

with a one-cylinder engine that always sounded like somebody
trying to flail their way out of an iron box with a brace of ball-
peen hammers. Gus didn't mind my owning the snowmobile at
all, strangely enough, but then it was used as a tool, not for recreation. From time to time Gus even used it himself to drag a
deer or to carry a load of furs out of the woods. It was those
helmeted, speed-crazed sports nuts who pissed Gus off, not
those who used snowmobiles to get the job done. Maybe "pissed
off" was too mild a term for it, considering what had happened.

I pulled the starter rope a couple of times, and the old Ski-
doo fired. Some seeds blew out of the throat of the muffler,
having been stored there by a mouse. With the garage quickly
filling with thick, bluish-grey exhaust fumes, I maneuvered the
snowmobile over to the side door and squeezed through it an
inch at a time, ripping loose some of the jamb, which fell in splin-
ters onto the greasy floor. Thumbing the chrome throttle lever,
I hauled around back of the sauna and, dodging clumps of brush
and stunted birch trees, glided toward an old, sand-filled railroad bed that had once served the logging industry in the 1890s
as a small-gauge spur used to haul out the white pine that had
been cut by the crews of hapless immigrants. There was no real
trail there any more, of course, but I knew the way, so the going
was fairly smooth. I dodged behind stands of popple, big
maples, and skirted around the occasional pin oak and numerous
spruce and red pine, managing, thereby, to stay out of sight of
our road—perhaps a needless precaution because visibility was
so bad due to the blowing snow that it would have been impossible for Norb, or even someone more alert, to see that far across
the fields and into the woods. By the time I made it to the old
highway, Nora was waiting. My parka and the front of my cap
were imprinted with a skin of white frost. Snow was stuck to my
coveralls. My face was nearly frozen, and my eyes were covered
with crystals that clung to my eyebrows and lashes. I hid the
snowmobile in a dense, brushy moraine half-filled with snow,
marking the spot with a long stick in case the machine disappeared beneath a drift.

Nora and I drove slowly to Watersmeet, found Fish Hatchery

Road, and, finally, the trailer, a rusty tin can of a dwelling with old cars and appliances in the yard, all of them bedded down in drifts. Smoke came out of the chimney in a stream that in the wind flew parallel to the roof. A bumper sticker proclaiming Red Power peeled from the front door.

"Well, the lovebirds," Gus shouted when he discovered who had knocked. "Come in and help me get ready."

"Gus," I said after a pause of a few seconds. I didn't really know what to say to him. Had he heard about the death of the snowmobiler? Since nobody else was there, I felt free to talk. "Did you hear that they're charging you with murder?" He looked very old and frail. His color was a ghastly white.

"Manslaughter," he snapped, "not murder. Dan heard it on his CB radio. They're putting her into high gear, but they'll never find me. Not this time." He grinned and then appeared thoughtful. Perhaps there was a slight possibility of his remaining free; we were dealing with the law after all. "They'll never make the charges stick. That guy was already in bad shape; they can't blame me."

I looked at Nora, and she shook her head sadly. What was the point to try to get Gus to listen to reason? On the way over to the reservation she had again mentioned that it would be best if Gus would go into the nursing home, which would mean that he would have to turn himself in and then deal with the hearings and such that would follow. I had told her to go ahead and try to talk to him—at least mention it to him as one option—but apparently she had decided not to. Gus was like a snowball gathering speed and mass as it rolled downhill. And he was bound, by an almost gravitational law, to complete his descent. Into what, I didn't know. But I had my suspicions. He looked like death only slightly warmed over.

Gus talked little while he packed his packsack, busily moving about, concentrating, mumbling—just like the old days when he would take off for a week or two in the woods. Finally he said, "Where's my parka?"

"The sheriff has it."

"What? That potlicker thinks he can keep my good coat?

Tell him to buy his own coat; doesn't he make enough money without stealing from poor people?"

Hopeless indeed, I thought, and it occurred to me that I had never thought of Gus as poor, let alone as a member of a category, though he certainly had few material possessions and virtually no money. "They're holding it for evidence," I offered mildly, but he just responded with a growl and continued packing. I was surprised to see a couple of lengths of rope and a fairly heavy block and tackle. What in hell did he have in mind now?

Just then a knock came on the door, and I nearly jumped out of my skin. Nora became grim and apprehensive. Gus just laughed, amused at our displays of paranoia. The door opened, and a big Indian fellow came in, followed by another, smaller man. They were both bundled up in red and black buffalo-checkered wool coats, navy blue stocking hats, green wool pants, Sorel boots and leather choppers. I recognized both of them, and we greeted one another. They were the men who had figured largely in a major incident that had befallen Gus several years before and was a turning point in his life . . . and in mine.

On a blizzardy night in 1985, while Gus was on the back leg of a round-trip poaching expedition, he wrapped his aluminum canoe around the rocks on the Fourteen Mile. Like some besotted Jonah he was cast up on the river's shore ice, half-drowned and frozen, but miraculously alive. The furs and carcasses he carried were lost; the canoe was flattened and bent almost in two by the force of the rushing water; and later Gus had to have two toes amputated at the hospital due to frostbite. Lying there in the slush and muck, helpless as a newborn bear cub, he was found by Eddie and Dan, both of them holy men of some kind—shamans or whatever—who happened to be camping in the area.

I forgot what Gus said they were doing there—looking for eagle feathers or birch bark or something like that. In any event, they said finding him was a great spiritual sign and that Gus was no longer the old Gus but had been reborn. I remember I teased him, saying that he was so tough and nasty tasting that even the river didn't want him, and Gus had gotten really angry, telling me I was an ignorant Finlander who didn't know anything about spiritual things and why didn't I just shut up if I couldn't say anything nice. Had I grown accustomed to this Gus? It was sure news to me that Gus was any more knowledgeable about things ineffable. Anyway, after Gus got out of the hospital in Ontonagon, Dan and Eddie came out to the farm and took him to a peyote ceremony somewhere over in Wisconsin, or maybe it was in Canada—I was never sure where they went—and he got free of the curse of alcohol. Just like that! Fifty years of being a drunk and . . . ZOT! Born again. It was scary. I liked the old Gus better. He began a fortunately brief career as a raving teetotaler, backing up his sobriety with, of all things, the Bible, some verses from which he scrawled with the burnt ends of kindling sticks on the kitchen walls at the farm. Well, total abstinence was not for him, and I was relieved when he started drinking again, although he never really hit the bottle hard after that. But Dan and Eddie would come and pick him up, and they'd be gone a few days at a time.

Once, when he came back, he told me that he had talked with a beaver who told him that his poaching days were over and that he had to start giving something back to the woods which had provided him with life. Gus figured out that Old Beaver, as he called him, wanted him to be an environmentalist. So he took the Green Road: War against the snowmobilers, joggers, campers, ORV jockeys and hikers. He quit selling fur, fish and game and instead just poached for food or some necessity—like when he needed a pelt for some project or other. And he still occasionally popped a cow that had escaped a pasture and strayed into the woods when he wanted some beef or felt like getting some sinew for re-stringing the webbing on his snowshoes.

Dan and Eddie stood by the door smiling nervously at Nora and me as they exchanged words with Gus. I couldn't figure out what the three of them were talking about, and, when I tried to inject myself into the conversation, Gus told me pointedly to shut up and carry his stuff out to Nora's truck. Nora followed me out, and we sat waiting, silence filling the Bronco. Gus eventually came out of the trailer, followed by Dan and Eddie. They all got into the Bronco, and Nora turned it around in the yard and headed back down the road to the highway.

Gus wanted to go back to the farm but decided that it would be unwise with the new warrant out. Surely the police were out in force. On the other hand, with the weather being what it was, their attention might be on the numerous fender-benders that always accompanied winter windstorms. I was surprised that Gus was apparently not trying to leave the U.S., or even the county. In fact, he talked only of getting back into the woods. I thought he wanted to go to Barking Bear or one of his other camps, which would have been crazy because surely those places were under surveillance by the authorities. But when we passed through Bruce Crossing, Gus told Nora to stop at the Baltimore River. The three of them got out, and Gus hefted his backpack up, a single strap hooked over his shoulder. We were parked off the road in the shelter of the bridge, and we watched them as they put on their snowshoes.

When Gus stood up, he looked at Nora. "You know, Miss Paavola, this Harry is no good for you."

She glanced at me and then turned back to Gus. "Yes, Mr. Haalakaa," she answered sweetly, "I know. Where are you going?"

"Where we all go," he laughed. "But that Harry there. . . ." He glowered at me and pointed a crooked finger, ". . . he doesn't know what he wants, unless it's just a maid, somebody to boss around. He doesn't do nothing but just watch the Christmas trees grow. Then he cuts them down already. He's got a problem."

"I'm quite aware of that, Mr. Haalakaa," Nora replied.

A car went over the bridge, and Gus glanced up at it and then said, "He's a goddamned fool."

She turned to me, expressionless, then back to Gus. "Yes," she said. I thought at first that she was just playing along with him, but now I wasn't sure. They were talking about me like I wasn't even there. I couldn't decide if I should protest, so I just stared at them in amazement, too numb to be hurt. A ball of clay formed in the pit of my stomach. My temples throbbed, and I felt the blood rush to my feet. I could feel myself grinding my teeth, and, with all my might, I resisted bursting into tears. Damn!

"But he's a good boy, that Harry," Gus added with a twinkle.

"Yes," she said and took my hand in both of hers.

"You're welcome," Gus said to me. "She's the only one who can fix you, Harry. I seen a long time already, a long, long time, and so I bait the trap and you come just like a wolf." He laughed wickedly.

"What are you saying? What am I thanking you for this time?" This guy had some nerve.

"I shot those snowmobiles to get you to wake up, you block-head," he snorted. "Now you got a woman, you can live like a human being instead of a mole hiding underground."

"What would you know about Nora and me?" I said, and I was going to say a lot more, but Nora, who was still holding my hand, squeezed until I thought the bones would crack. When I shut up, she relaxed her grip. I looked at her.

"Mr. Haalakaa, I don't think I like the sound of this," she said, a playful melodiousness in her voice.

"Youse the smart one, all right," he said. "I was up at the farm last night with Dan and Eddie. We come down the drive in neutral with the lights off—that stupid Norbert sleeping in his car up on the road didn't even see us—and when we see the house dark and that Bronco there, I tell these guys that ding nephew of mine finally found a good use for that old pump handle of his."

"Jesus Christ, Gus," I whined. I was completely embarrassed. "What were you doing on the farm anyway? It's a wonder you didn't get picked up." Apart from the voyeuristic implications of his confession, which I was not going to touch, i was amazed at his seeming lack of concern for the latter contingency. If he wanted to stay free, and, by all the hiding out he had done, it appeared that he did, shouldn't he be in Florida by now?

"We had some business to take care of in the woods," Gus said matter of factly. "It took all night, and it was hard work, too." He puffed up and mugged for me.

"What business?" I asked. I was afraid it had something to

do with poaching.

He chuckled and shook his finger at me again. "You be finding out . . . but not now."

"Nora, let's get out of here," I said. God, I was getting frightened on top of embarrassed. What would Gus say or do next? The only predictable thing about him was that it could be anything, which of course was what it was. He leaned through the open door of the Bronco, and, closing his eyes once he had his target sighted in, he gave Nora a big wet kiss on the lips. She kissed him back, and I felt a peal of jealousy ring throughout my nervous system.

"Are you sure you set this whole thing up for Harry, Mr. Haalakaa?" she purred.

He smiled like a barn cat at milking time and kissed her again. "Ah," he said, "you come with me, and we go to Florida instead of the woods."

"Okay," she said with a laugh. She looked at me, and I felt instantly reassured.

"No, you better stay and take care of this big kid."

"Whatever you say, Mr. Haalakaa."

"And you can call me Gustav now, I think," he said.

He reached into the truck and patted me on the shoulder with a mittened hand. "Now when Dan and Eddie come for you, you got to go with them already . . . understand?"

"What?" I said.

"You make him go," he said to Nora.

"I will," she replied.

"Where are you going, Gus?"

At that moment a group of six or so ravens flew by us, taking a quick look at the people who had decided to stop by the highway bridge, which was no doubt a good scavenging spot for the carcasses of animals hit by cars. Gus pointed at the ravens. "I'm going with them," he said.

So Gus left with Dan and Eddie, and Nora took me through Ewen and out onto the old highway to where my snowmobile was parked. On the way we talked about what they could be up to, speculating and wondering and finally having to give up. All the crazy things I had ever heard about everybody else's relatives seemed to pale before this. As I watched Nora pull away—she had decided to check the farm and Haalakaa Road for cops and then call me later from her place—I felt a pang of remorse for having slept with her. I was paying now for the price of involvement—the pain of separation, which was not at all unfamiliar to me.

When I got back to the farm, there was a note on the door to call Tony Coelho at the Sheriff's Department. I stumped into the kitchen, dropping snow and ice everywhere, and dialed the number. The dispatcher answered, and, when I told her who I was, she said Tony was very angry as it was now generally believed that I was helping Gus. Tony said as much when he came on the line, plus that they were going to charge me with aiding in the commission of assorted felonies too numerous to count and too serious to talk about over the phone. Tony sounded positively steamed, and I guessed that the Feds and the DNR must have been putting his feet to the fire in order to get him to make an arrest. While he scoffed at their scientific methods, their bureaucratic style, and their big city talk, I think he was probably just covering up his own feelings of being a backwoods yokel; he sensed that they were laughing at him and looking down on him as a hick sheriff who couldn't catch a flea even if he buggared a muskrat. As for me, he was going to stretch my hide over a rain barrel and turn me into a bass drum if he could prove that I had helped Gus. Rumor had it, he said, that Gus was still around.

"You remember that time he went into the river and them two bow and arrows from Watersmeet fished him out of the water?"

Panic! Gulp . . . "Uh, yeah."

"What were their names? Didn't he hang around with them a bit after that? I recall a deputy stopping them one time on the highway."

"I . . . I . . . don't remember."

"Don't remember or don't want to remember?"

"Honest, Tony, I. . . ."

"Harry, don't fuck with me, I'm warning you, this is no game

70

now. Gus killed a guy. . . ."

"Come on, Tony, you know he didn't kill anybody. That warrant is just an excuse to expend the man hours looking for him. The Feds and the DNR just want to look good."

"Like I said, Harry, don't mess with me. I want Gus, and you better either give him to me or stay out of the way so we can get him. I mean it. You'll find your dumb Finlander ass in jail. Do you hear me?"

Was I deaf? Of course I could hear him. He was yelling his head off. Amazing. Even more amazing was the fact that a wonderful calm seemed to fill me. I was completely at peace, clear-headed even.

6

Late that afternoon it started snowing again, heavily this time. Within an hour we had six inches and, by the time it was dark, over a foot. I turned on the radio and heard that the Michigan State Police had closed the highway that ran through the U.P. along Lake Superior. I listened to a news brief about Gus, now being sought in connection with the death of Robert Lindstrom, aged fifty-two, of Harbor Springs, Michigan, who had collapsed and died after the business with the snowmobiles in the woods—an incident being billed as a sniper attack. The phone rang, and Tony wanted to know if I was ready to turn Gus in. I got angry and told him to take his warrant and shove it. Fuck him, I thought, beyond caring whether I was going to be charged with aiding a fugitive. But the longer I thought about it, the more I worried about that rifle out in that old washing machine, although maybe Gus had picked it up by now. Of course, I wondered what would happen if the police or whoever ran into him while he was "armed and dangerous," which was how the news broadcast had characterized him.

After I ate a supper of bacon and eggs, the phone started ringing every five minutes or so. Concerned citizens, most of them friends of Gus, claimed to know where Gus was, wanted to help, or just wanted to get the story straight so they could add their two cents to the rumor mill. About half the people who called asked me if it was true that Nora and I were now a couple, and wasn't that just wonderful, and had we set a wedding date. I was struck dumb with embarrassment. There was not a whole lot of privacy in that neck of the woods. Had it not been for the fact that I was waiting for Nora to call, I would have taken the phone off the hook. But as it was, I couldn't bring myself to do it. Around ten, by which time I was half in the bag from a fifth of brandy, Nora phoned to say she had tried to call me about ten times, but the line was always busy. She had also tried to come out to the farm as planned to see what the police were up to, but Haalakaa Road was drifted and she got stuck. Norb had been cruising the area, found her and pulled her out, so she ended up back home, one of those cabin-in-a-kit places just north of Bruce Crossing.

"I love you, Nora," I blurted out, surprised at the sound of my voice which seemed like that of a stranger, not to mention the words which I hadn't uttered since maybe the fifth grade when I made a clumsy pass at a little girl who was staying for the summer up the road from Grandpa's farm at the Johnsons. She had laughed at me and said that she would never love a stinky country boy and was going to marry a boy she knew named Ringo. Nora was less cruel, but I couldn't help but feel stupid. Telling her I loved her elicited a laugh. Poor me.

"Will I see you tomorrow?" I asked.

"I don't know," she replied. "I have to go to Marquette if the highway is clear."

"What for?" I bleated, an embarrassing croak in my voice.

"Don't worry, Harry. I'll call you when I get back."

I was drunk and exhausted when I crawled up to bed. I lay face down on the pillow and breathed in. It was still there; the aroma of morels in spring, washed with the sweet water of birch: Nora. In my mind was the picture of whirling springs bubbling

up from sandy-bottomed, creek-side pools. Our bodies entwined, suspended in spiraling blue and copper prisms. My God!
Nora, whom I knew but didn't really know that well, whom I had
made love to, or with—or slept with—or whatever I was supposed to call it. Better still, what did it mean?

My mouth was dry, but, when I tried to get up to get a drink
of water, I got dizzy and so decided to just lie there and try to
sleep. The snow stopped briefly and the moon rose, sending
beams of opaque, bluish-white light into the room. I looked out
and could see stars above the southern horizon. If I traced her
name in the constellations, would she be mine forever? Or if I
found her in the features of the moon? Having sunk into a near-
mythic intoxication, I imagined that now I would never lose her.
Surely a case for the padded room, complete with buckled
lounging robe, leather harness and rubber bit.

Who was she? Nora Saima Paavola. Age thirty-eight, or did
she say thirty-six? Five-six, one hundred fifteen pounds. (My
estimate.) Raven-black hair and eyes. Size six-and-a-half shoe.
(Her estimate.) Very good looking, I should say. Modest propor-
tions overall but in impeccable physical relation to one another,
including a great ass which I had submitted to unobtrusive mea-
surement for years. Pale complexion—radiating the energy of a
night person trapped in a day job; hence the coffee and cigarettes
to provide needed adrenal assistance. Thin, somewhat heron-
like, but strong, and bordering on the aerobically muscular.
Good teeth. (Braces in childhood?) Apart from smoking, no habits
or visible scars . . . which vision was followed by my discovery
that by thinking about her in this way it was becoming almost
taxonomical, or, in keeping with my paranoia, autopsy-ish.

I shook my head to try to clear away this objective picture,
reflecting instead on her voice and her story. Lying there wrapped
in the sheets, smoking cigarettes without the slightest concession
to the folly of wanton disregard of country home safety, whis-
pering in her almost hoarse voice, she told me about her childhood and the latter days, which was the first time I had heard
the story in one breath.

Previously when she came out to see Gus, I was sometimes

able to get her to talk about herself, but it was like pulling teeth. I had thought that she was sort of Finn-typically self-effacing and, therefore, uncomfortable calling attention to herself by letting me know anything about her. But our first time together she explained that she had gotten sick of trying to justify to people why she had never married, and didn't care if they thought she was a dyke or had something wrong with her. I was touched by her almost sympathetic understanding of the people who assume a woman should be married, and can't imagine that someone might make this choice not to be—or else refuse to settle for the kind of toxic male rubble available in quantity in the upper midwest.

She was born in Hancock, a normal middle class girl out of parents who were second generation Finn. They were both teachers and fortunately only part-time Lutherans, so she had not been particularly frozen in place, which is the lot of many. She took piano lessons, sold Girl Scout cookies, broke her elbow ice skating, and lost her virginity via what would now be called date-rape to a football player after the homecoming game her freshman year of high school. She was the salutatorian of her class, losing the valedictorian title by a hair to a girl who later died of leukemia. She went to Michigan Tech as a prospective engineering student but then transferred to Northern in Marquette, where she majored in social work as she wanted to help people rather than work on submarines, dams or H-bombs, or, for that matter, design pole buildings for the local pissant businessmen/developers. After graduating, she got some sort of job working with the Indians at L'Anse, then went to Detroit, staying there for four years until breaking up with her fiancé, a guy she met at work, afterwards coming back to the north country for which she had longed while in the ghetto rat race. She settled, finally, in Bruce Crossing, where she conducted some of the state of Michigan's poverty business, which of course included keeping track of Uncle Gus.

Five or six serious boyfriends all told, including the fiancé who had hit her once, which was one too many times; plus a few "unserious" ones.

"Who's to say what's serious?" I had joked when she told me this.

She surprised me with a hard punch to the stomach that took away my air for a moment. As pretty and almost delicate as she seemed, there was a raw toughness there that made her seem as at home with quilting and canning as with guns and chainsaws, and, as she proved, a short right hook. She hunted grouse without dogs and she liked to fly fish, preferring dry flies, which she knew how to tie though she seldom had the time. A pretty good cook, but in the direction of breads, bakery and cakes, not dinners. Fond of novels, catalog shopping, video tapes (mostly artsy, or so it seemed to me, because I knew few of her favorites). She mentioned a few women friends from college whom she occasionally visited though they were scattered around the Midwest and the east coast. To keep herself sane during the winter, she sometimes helped coach girls' basketball, and she took lots of photographs, most of which remained undeveloped in film cans stored in her refrigerator. Unlike me, she had also traveled, including trips to Europe and northern Africa (Egypt). Dislikes: manipulative people, particularly men; bigots; tourists, though if you came and stayed in the U.P., she would go out of her way to get to know you and make you feel welcome. She didn't like the wariness and secrecy owned by small-town people, though she understood why they were reluctant to embrace the stranger.

Pillow talk was wonderful and at the same time dangerously intoxicating, a true aphrodisiac, though I couldn't identify one, since I tended to stick to the U.P.'s official national hallucinogen, alcohol—liberally sprinkled with pool, darts and bowling—which had the opposite effect. And again there was the memory of us lying with our heads together on the pillow, my hands lightly stroking her slender, almost skinny body, her fingers touching my lips, her eyes slightly closed with pupils dilated, still intently focused, but on some distant point. I entered her again and we came simultaneously, a testimony at least to our compatible body mechanics, if not to an evolving, increasingly whole, emotional unity.

But I remembered wondering immediately afterwards if it wasn't somehow a mistake. Then she cried, and I thought that something had happened or that something was wrong—or even that she had detected my equivocation—but she said no; she had known how beautiful it would be and how much she wanted me, but she was determined to put it off as long as possible until she knew it would be right and we couldn't miss. And now we couldn't—at least not without some serious self-delusion, at which people our age tend to be fairly accomplished. A big risk.

Recognizing myself in this vision of faked intimacy, I started asking her how she could have known what it would be like to make love with me, and why she couldn't avoid me any more, and did it ever really have anything to do with Gus. But she refused to answer and then pretended to sleep so that I would quit talking. Until then, Gus had been the only person to tell me to shut up. Nora had done it with a great deal more grace. I remember thinking: I like this, even if I'm not in control.

The sensation of being lost—an exalted state of dizziness and deja vu, of panic and wonder. This emotional landscape of retreating horizons and ambiguous vistas, of disappearing landmarks and melting shadows: Nora. I was lost. For real, if not for good.

I remembered a typical January day from my youth. It had been snowing hard. Gus had taken me with him on a trapping expedition but later left me at Barking Bear, telling me to stay put. I rustled around in his stuff—normally a fascinating adventure in a nether world of antique memorabilia and plain junk—but for some reason even the exotic wasn't living up to its billing that day. Bored and restless, I decided to go for a walk outdoors. I put on my woolen pants, sweater and cap, snugged up my parka and strapped on a pair of old snowshoes. By taking the rifle, I could claim that I had seen a rabbit, a necessary excuse, I believed, should Gus come back and find me gone. And gone I was. I walked out the door of the cabin and probably hadn't taken more than thirty steps when I got turned around. There was no need to look for a compass; since Gus didn't believe in them, I didn't own one either, though it might have been put to good use just then. Snow tumbled down in streams of starry flakes, covering my tracks, bending over trees and branches, and utterly transforming the landscape. It was the first time I had really ever been lost. In my forgetful state of total surrender, I peed down both legs. So much for everything I had learned up to then. I ran first in one direction, then in another looking for some sort of familiar sign, but I could just as easily have been on the moon. I was totally disoriented and half-crazed with exhaustion and fear. By dark I was wet, cold and weepy.

It stopped snowing finally, and the moon came out, which allowed me to see a little—much to my great, albeit temporary, relief—the previous two hours of coming darkness having been particularly horrifying. I crossed the tracks I had made earlier, though how much earlier I couldn't say. In any case, they always seemed to be heading in the wrong direction.

At last, I was truly desperate. I had not wanted to fire the rifle three times in rapid succession, the universal distress signal; in fact, I wanted to die first, because Gus always said that this signal was for life and death emergencies only, not for the kind of minor trouble people get themselves into in the woods—getting temporarily lost being one of them. Well, what could I do? I fired the rifle, and no sooner had the orange flame of the last shot torn a hole in the sparkling blue-black curtain of the vast northern sky and echoed endlessly through the forest labyrinth, than I saw a dim light peeping through the thickly painted branches of the snow-laden trees. Looking down the golden bar of light to its twinkling source, I could see the kitchen window of Camp Barking Bear. As I stumbled closer, I could see Gus' head as he bustled about inside. I had been walking in circles around the camp for hours. I was embarrassed down to my frozen toes and hated myself for being such a dim-bulb, the upshot of which was that I couldn't force myself to go inside. I was certainly afraid of Gus' wrath—he didn't countenance disobedience—but mostly I dreaded something far worse: ridicule. So I stood and shivered and cried and swore. Some time passed, and Gus opened the door finally and said in that ironic manner of his, "Well, are youse going to stay out there all night, or do I get a little help skinning these damn beaver?"

"I'll help you," I said after I got over the shock of hearing a human voice other than my own after a day of terror-stricken solitude. So I went in, and Gus gave me some cold rice and canned prunes, plus some fried beaver tail and a big slug of whiskey—the latter even though I was only fourteen years old at the time. Later that evening, after I had warmed up and we sat at the big table flensing the raw hides, Gus reached over to a shelf and picked up a ball of sisal twine, which he tossed to me. "What's this for?" I asked.

"The next time youse go out maybe tie one end to your belt loop and the other to a chair leg." That was all he ever said about it or all he ever had to say. I never got lost again—not in the woods, anyway.

In life . . . a different story. I felt incredibly worn out, as tired as I had been when I had been lost and kept running across my own tracks—dizzy, visions of things being misplaced, of the world turned upside down—lost in the endless, vibrant wilderness landscape of . . . Nora.

I slept and then had a vivid dream: Gus as a hanged man, only the gallows was a snarewire around his neck beneath a lean-to shelter at the base of a giant red pine. Ravens in the surrounding trees, their terrible cries filling my head like shards of glass from an exploding window. Eddie and Dan, the two shamans, watching me like statues with animated eyes, sitting crosslegged on either side of Gus.

I leapt up out of the dream to the unreality of consciousness; terrified, soaked through with sweat and carrying a terrific headache besides. Very carefully I eased myself into a standing position and made it to the kitchen. I took a couple of aspirin with a glass of water. Shaking uncontrollably, I spilled water all over the floor.

While I mopped it up with a dish towel, I noticed the sound, which seemed to be coming more from inside my head than from outside. Had I heard it in my dream also? A coyote? A big dog? Perhaps even a wolf, although this would have been most rare. Whatever it was, it was quite close to the house and was madly cutting loose with arias of cascading, tooth-loosening howls. I ran to the kitchen window and saw an animal close to the garage. Gray and huge, with a corona of white fur encircling its head. My God, a timber wolf! I couldn't believe it at first and kept closing my eyes and opening them, expecting it to go away. But it stayed.

I had seen a wolf only once before, and that had been what was called a "possible sighting": no one believed me at the time. Now I looked at the creature, awe-struck, breathless and fixated. Was it sick? Lost? Did wolves get lost? I had never seen or heard that a wolf would approach humans, let alone come into someone's yard—except in the movies perhaps.

In the U.P. only the horror stories cooked up by aged braggarts remained. Wolves had become dangerous spirits in the minds of those who had listened to the older generation—worse than bears, because at least bears were still around and anyone who encountered one knew they weren't particularly dangerous. But wolves, being rare, still sent chills up the spine, which was why people tended to shoot them on sight despite the DNR's efforts to educate the populace as to their basically benign character.

Everyone said Gus had killed the last wolf in the U.P., although now they were supposedly coming back, being reintroduced. Anyway, this wolf was in full voice and refused to stop— even when I opened the back door and threw a chunk of firewood at it. All it did was move off out of my range and commence to get even louder. At first I was excited, then scared, then puzzled. It was very alarming besides. Finally, still drunk and exhausted, I decided it didn't matter and went back to bed.

The goddamned wolf found my window and sat right beneath it on a frozen, three-foot-deep snowdrift, wailing for all he was worth. I unstuck the frosted sash, ripped open the storm window and threw pieces of wood from the bedroom, running down to the kitchen several times to replenish my supply of missiles. It deftly dodged my best shot.

By the time I had to get out of bed the third time, I was in a blind rage. Cursing and screaming and throwing things had not worked, so I ran downstairs to the kitchen and took down my .22 from the gunrack. I was in a completely irrational state but somehow decided against a larger caliber, thinking that I might ruin the pelt. I also remember thinking that no one would blame me for shooting the sonofabitch, that the various statutes, federal and state, which added up to about a hundred years in the pen and the sacrifice of the first born for twenty generations, wouldn't apply in my case, the Code of the Woods taking precedent whenever an animal interfered with one's sleep. Or whatever. Anyway, I went back into the bedroom, tore open the window and fired a quick shot. The wolf jumped straight up in the air, curled into a tight, hairy ball, and on landing let out the most anguished cry I ever heard. It stumbled through a snowdrift that transected the yard, howling in pain.

The rifle was only a single shot, and I had to rush back into the kitchen to find some more shells, not even thinking that I should use a larger caliber weapon. The wolf was still outside by the time I had the rifle loaded. I fired again, this time out of the kitchen window. Again the wolf leapt straight into the air and came back down—still crying, but now even louder than before. Then, apparently retreating at last, it dragged itself to the edge of the yard from where it continued its howling. Losing sight of it, but hearing its agonized cries, I realized that I would have to go outside and try to finish it off.

I dressed quickly, although there was no hurry as I could still hear it, and then I went out into the deep, fresh snow. I sank nearly to my thighs and fought the drifts across the yard, finding my way by flashlight. I saw the wolf near one of the thorn apple trees opposite the wellspring and fired, but missed. It moved off a little, and I reloaded.

I was completely panicked, shaking all over. What had I done? Had anybody been watching the house? What would I do with the body, the pelt, my fractured mind when this was all over? If it would ever end. . . .

It was to happen over and over again. I would follow its cries, finally overtake it, try a shot, miss and follow it once again into the thick woods, but 'round and 'round in big circles. What kind of madman would do this? What kind of greenhorn, tender-foot sonofabitch? Violator of natural laws, or the Code. My bellows and curses echoed in the trees. Why had I shot it in the first place? What ignorance, or, more likely, perverted predatory instinct, had led me to try to kill it? Once I wounded it though, I had to kill it. What was it that the Code said: Beware the dangerous loss of control. Then the woods went silent, and I lost the wolf's tracks in a cedar swamp down by the South Branch.

Either it was dead or else had simply disappeared. In the deep snow which covered the tangled floor of the swamp, the flashlight cast long shadows that confused me. I tried a random, criss-cross search pattern, a hopeless effort, following first one set of tracks, then another before realizing that they were either made by deer or by me.

At dawn I came close to another one of Gus' camps, about a half-mile from the farm, and decided to try to collect myself. The camp, called Workman's Comp, was where Gus kept most of the tools of his trade—traps, guns, bait, extra whiskey and I don't know what all. For a moment I wondered if Gus himself might be there, but then I realized that this was unlikely; it was too near the farm. The building was two ten-by-ten WPA drying shacks that had been bolted together and sided and roofed with tin. Gus considered it his only benefit from the government's Depression programs for the unemployed. Gus had stolen it in a caper involving a borrowed flatbed truck equipped with a winch. Nestled among snow-covered trees, its stovepipe bent over slightly; it looked like any old shack in the woods, except that U.S. Government Property was stenciled in blue paint all over the interior walls.

I was so happy to be there that I momentarily forgot all about that goddamned wolf—or whatever it was. I was beginning to think the whole thing had been a nightmare. When I got inside the camp, I found it deserted, of course, except for mice and the weasel Gus called Hairy Legs, a white, onyx-eyed character who was fat and tame. I thought that H.L. might be a vegetarian, since he rarely bothered the mice, although he had probably just gotten used to Gus' table scraps and an occasional raw egg.

I took off my parka and cap, hung up my mittens to dry on a nail by the stovepipe, and brushed off my clothes, letting the snow and ice fly around the room. I was in a sorry state. Beyond exhaustion or even depression, and worried in the vague sort of way that haunted a person who had stepped out of bounds and could see what he had done, I knew I couldn't retrace my steps. It was like the time I had shot a yearling buck. I was suddenly overtaken by remorse and fought down an urge to follow the path along which it had traveled to encounter my bullet, as if I could return to its source and find it there still alive, owning a different fate should it see me in time. I was prone to such reveries; Gus told me that they lasted for days.

I leaned against the wall and, some time later, found myself tracing a finger over the stenciled lettering and realized that the Feds, the DNR and the sheriff might be on their way out to the farm. And I thought of Nora. Could she possibly be of any help if Gus were to get caught, or if I wound up charged with a crime or crimes? Undoubtedly. Maybe. It could be that she was now out of the loop, as they say, having triggered the sheriff's intuitive distrust for civilians and do-gooders.

Dozens of cops could be all over the woods at that very moment, I thought, or four of them at any rate, as they always went around in matching pairs hereabouts: One to screw in the light bulb, two to work the rubber hose and the last one to testify before the legislature on behalf of a bigger budget. Well, let them come. Gus could out-fox these stooges all winter long, and, if he so desired, for good.

But Gus was eighty-one. Congestive heart failure loomed; slowly inflating, his heart would some day implode. Perhaps it already had with all the excitement and exertion. Or maybe he would turn himself in and be done with it. Face the music, as they say. Did *sisu*—what the Finns call nerve or guts—diminish with the disillusionment born of decay? Or was this just more of the nonsense pop nostalgia that sold bran cereals and rowing machines these days? Gus had put six snowmobiles in the junkyard after all, and one man in his casket—if someone wanted to include that guy's dying, which I surely did not. From ashes to ashes. Maybe Gus would plink some of the cops with his .243, if he had thought to retrieve it from the washing machine. If he had really flipped his bark hat, that is.

I imagined that Tony would come out to the farm, arrest me, and push me ahead of the posse to take the first shot if Gus put the party in the cross-hairs of his Leupold 3x9 power variable scope, a nifty apparatus I had bought him the previous fall, hoping that he would like it too much to risk losing it in a poaching bust. And after Gus had shot me in the heart, would he pick off the others like grackles on a wire fence? He might.

Or maybe it would go the other way along the lines of a contra ambush employing television-like S.W.A.T. team fire-power: They would lure the old boar out with his dying nephew as bait and then gun down the both of us. Or better still, corner him at Barking Bear and push me in the door ahead of them: Gunfire, smoke, an upturned table, and I would stagger outside, making red candy canes on the icy stoop. Hollywood haiku. No thanks. I vowed when I got back to the farm I would call Tony and tell him everything, that imaginary confessional doing my bruised brain some temporary good.

I smoked several cigarettes in a row from a pack I had mooched from Nora, drank a little water and felt better by and by. It was a beautiful day after all. The wind-blown clouds formed a luminous silver web across the deep pool of the sky. Ah, pseudo-poetry. My erection throbbed. If only I played guitar. And if only I hadn't shot that damned wolf. What did it mean? It didn't take a lot of literary imagination to recognize that this was some sort of cosmically ordained event, some grand epiphany. Then came a stroke-like realization that brought me up short. Nora and I were a couple; we were together. I couldn't swallow for several anxious minutes. How was it, as they say, for her? Had she realized this, too? I decided to stay at Workman's Comp for a while and soon fell asleep on the tick mattress on the bunk, waking quickly on dreaming of the cruelly wounded wolf mechanically licking its wounds, slowly stiffening in the cold, its yellow eyes rheumy and passive with impending death. I quickly dressed and went back to the farm, leaving the camp open as dictated by the Code of the Woods. And just precisely what did the Code have to say about shooting wolves—and then losing them? Save one shot for yourself, you potlicker.

When I got to the top of the sandhill railroad grade east of the house I saw an old car parked in the driveway. Smoke poured out of the sauna chimney. It had to be Gus . . . or was it some sort of trap to lure me back home? Approaching warily, I finally decided that it was probably some friend of Gus' come either to help or to claim that Gus owed him money. As I made my way over the frozen creek that ran hard near the sauna, plowing snow with my knees, Eddie and Dan, Gus' Indian buddies, opened the sauna door and stepped outside, naked as two newborn mice. A giant cloud of steam belched from the interior of the little cabin. Dan smiled. Eddie nodded. I left my coat and rifle on the elm chopping block outside the door and followed them inside.

"You get him?" Dan asked as I undressed.

"Who do you mean? Gus?" I answered.

Eddie laughed, his long face curling into a mask of wrinkles. He slapped his bare thigh. "The wolf."

"We seen the tracks," said Dan, "Big wolf, but you didn't hit him too good."

My head was spinning. The heat, even in the dressing room, which was separate from the sauna, was unbearable. I had trouble getting my pants off, which were damp from snow and sweat. "No . . . I . . . didn't . . . I wasn't trying to. . . ." I left off; it was impossible to explain.

They looked at one another. "That's okay," said Dan. "We'll find him for you."

"How much?" asked Eddie.

"Huh? How much what?" I replied.

"How much you asking for the pelt?" said Dan.

"The pelt? No . . . I. . . ."

"Ten thousand dollars and a year in jail," Eddie, straight-faced, interrupted. There was a pregnant pause, and then they both roared with laughter.

7

Sauna, sweat-lodge, steam bath—all the same. The walls dripping, the steam flowing through one's body, merging memory with present; visions of ancestors and friends, of the wolf, raven, beaver, tribe, the living, the dead. I melted into the bench and stared at the ceiling through the fog as the vapors erased my pain: Nora, Gus, the tree-farm, Dan and Eddie, the sheriff, anonymous cops in leather and steel, Dad, Mom, Grandpa, and Grandmother. The dead snowmobiler. Eddie singing a sad Indian song. A death song, Dan said. For Gus.

A couple of hours passed and then we stood naked outside before getting dressed so that our skin would be dry, the cold driving the blood back down into our bodies from the surface of our skin where it had flowed to protect us against the infernal, searing heat. "Where's Gus?" I asked them.

"We took him," said Dan somberly.

"Took him where?"

"To his death place," said Eddie as he rubbed snow on his barrel chest.

We went back inside and finished drying ourselves with a towel. It was still hot in the changing room, and we struggled to pull on our clothes.

"Where is he?" I asked again.

They looked at each other. "Gus said not to tell you," Dan said softly. He was a little embarrassed.

"Not to tell me? Why not?"

Eddie grinned. "You have to find him if you want to see him."

"I don't understand."

"Your uncle Gus could talk to animals, you know that?" said Eddie.

"I . . . guess, but . . . I. . . ."

"And they talked to him," offered Dan.

"Ho!" Eddie exclaimed.

"We left the block and tackle there but you should take it down after . . ." said Dan.

"After what?" I asked.

"After you have a look . . . then in the spring you go back and . . ." Eddie said. "He said he didn't care what you did after that." He laughed. "You understand?"

I nodded, but I wasn't getting it. We were dressed, and I walked with them to their car, a rusty, '60s vintage Ford Galaxy 500 with a cracked windshield and crinkled hood. It bore no license plate, and the grill was broken. The door hinge groaned when Eddie got in behind the wheel. Dan stood with me and put a hand on my shoulder. "Go find him. He honors you with a gift."

"Gift? What gift?" I asked. Gus didn't have a thing in this world; what could he give me? Ah, I thought, maybe his rifle, or. . . .

"Ho!" Eddie called from inside the car. He pumped the accelerator a few times and then fired the mufflerless engine, which let out a surprised gasp and then exploded into a growly rumble, punctuated with loud backfires. As the car throbbed and chugged, puffing blue smoke, Dan climbed in. I watched as Eddie fishtailed the big car around, and it slowly sledded up the long s-curve of the snow-bound driveway. Apparently the snowplow had come late the night before or else early that morning while I was still out at Workman's Comp Camp, though there was still some drifting to contend with. I watched them turn the corner onto our road. A horn sounded. I waved, but they were already out of sight.

I went into the house and found it ice-cold, but fortunately the water pipes hadn't frozen. I built a fire in the barrel stove in the basement and another in the kitchen, but it was quite a while before the house warmed up. I was hungry and made some scrambled eggs with venison sausage. There was a little brandy left in the jug from the night before, and I finished it off with water—"hair of the god," as Gus called it. Demon is more like it, but it did the trick, and my hangover lifted, enabling me to at least try to puzzle everything out. The sauna had removed most of my furies, leaving only the stark realities to be faced. Or should I say Reality? Gus.

Nora was in Marquette, I guessed, because she didn't answer her phone. I hated answering machines, so when it came on every time I rang her, I just hung up. Telephone-itis.

A gift . . . what gift? I was annoyed with Eddie and Dan; they had seemed so cryptically bemused. I had nothing against them, but these guys had always seemed "other," never quite standing on the same ground with anyone. Whether it was a superior attitude, or, more likely, their scheming shamanic ways, it was all the same to me. They could have told me what had happened to Gus, and, the more I thought about it, the angrier I got.

I decided to try to just forget the whole thing—my usual style—but I quickly realized that if I did that on this occasion, I would never really know what had happened. I would have to see it through. I wondered about the wolf for a while but decided that Eddie and Dan would handle that matter. God, what a fool I was sometimes.

Nora would be back in the evening. The house was warm again. Out of brandy. I put wood in the woodbox and changed my clothes. I put on some water to boil for coffee and tried Nora again, this time leaving a message, which I never finished before the tape ended, leaving me frustrated all over again.

Where had they taken him? I would find him, they had said. But how? I watched more ravens flying down toward the river, thinking that the rookery there must be humongous, and wondering why I had never seen it before in my wanderings in the woods, although they often moved their gathering places as the availability of food dictated. I went out and did some serious shoveling, trying to at least free the garage and back porch from the snowdrifts, which, if they froze, would be like iron in a day or so. Of course this shoveling stuff was a sort of automatic reflex—like shooting a wolf on sight, in a way—and had to do with the way people were brought up; the look of a sidewalk, a driveway, a porch, stoop or entryway in winter was a sign of character . . . or lack of it. Out in the country, I didn't feel any compulsion to scrape everything clean of snow—thereby satisfying snoopy purists—just as I would shoot a damned wolf and then feel bad about it.

I worked up a worthy sweat pushing and tossing snow around and let the realization that Gus was dead take hold. What did that mean, exactly? It saddened me, but it was not that he was no more—or if that, not only that—no . . . more than that . . . there was something else besides. He had left a legacy too. The gift. But what gift? Gus had changed so much over my own lifetime. From drunk trapper and poacher to . . . what? Eco-warrior sounded too glitzy, and so did environmentalist. Obviously the biggest change had to do with Dan and Eddie who had saved him that time from the river and subsequently from the bottle. They had somehow given him a perspective that his own opportunistic, utilitarian orientation to the woods originally lacked. They had, in a sense, converted him, but to what? Thank God that Christian thing didn't last. Maybe it was more like sharing— the sharing of a vision of nature rather than a conversion. Every animal, tree, swamp and moon, every spring and bear's den, every stump and moraine was, after his experiences with Dan and Eddie, grounded in the totality of some new vision. It was a vision of the nations in nature: Of the two-leggeds, the four-leggeds, the swimming people and the flying people—each species with its own place and mode of existence, its own rights and obligations, its own relations with the other nations of a united nations of ecology. And Gus' own role—his own place—in nature changed. He was no longer just a top-of-the-food-chain kind of guy. He cared for the whole, was its benefactor. And this seemed to have become such a natural part of him, perhaps evidenced best by the fact that he no longer required alcohol to find his center. Up to then he had been strictly predatory, drunk and disorderly, part of the lost second generation of Finns who were missing not so much a sense of place as a sense or a feeling of belonging, always in conflict with themselves, always at odds with people or nature, or both.

Or the law, I thought, and wondered when the cops would show with guns drawn. I pictured the victim of Gus' so-called sniper attack laid out in his crinoline-lined casket, hovered over by a sobbing, bovine widow, their clutch of round-headed kids sullenly observing the wax-job done on their dad by the mortician, secretly plotting revenge on society. I felt badly about this, very badly. I smoked a cigarette and tried to remember something a little more pleasant—what Gus had said about being with Eddie and Dan on the reservation, sitting there cross-legged and naked in the sweat lodge, pouring water on fire-hot rocks; about meeting the Bear Guardian, giving prayers to Messenger Eagle, smoking Grandmother Pipe, learning the songs from Beaver. He hadn't told me much beyond this, except to say that the wigwam lodge, a smallish dome made of saplings, cedar boughs and canvas, was the equal of the best sauna in its capacity to produce mind-melting heat—that and the fact that he had learned to talk to animals there and now understood what everything in the woods was about. "I know what it means," he said.

At the time I dismissed that as so much hokum. I even ridiculed him, which I later regretted doing. But Gus praying? Give me a small break. Gus the rapt student of Indian lore? I couldn't imagine it. But everything seemed to point in that direction. Indians and Finns had only labored together but had never had any joint community involvements of which I was aware. But why not? Weren't the Finns coming out of some stone-age/

Lapland/reindeer herd/frozen tundra/mythic Arctic past that wasn't altogether different from the native experience, or at least akin enough to allow them to relate to native people? Think about it. Well, perhaps that's stretching it. Most likely Gus was just primed—primed for the experience by years of predation and self-destruction. Being crazy helped, too. On the other hand, maybe it was true that we who were not natives any more had much to learn from those who still were. Gus thought so, I guess.

Not that it mattered much now. I was exhausted, so I lay down and must have fallen asleep instantly. The only dream was of the wolf being picked to pieces by ravens. When I awoke, it was nearly five o'clock in the evening and already dark out. I ate, threw an extra sandwich into my Duluth pack along with a bottle of water and put on my parka. I soon bumped along on the Ski-doo on one of Gus' minimalist trails that were his signature. The headlight bounced and flickered, and I strained to see where I was going. In reality, his so-called trails were just blazes on a stick or branch here and a few pebbles in a pile or a bent bush there. Very Indian, come to think of it. In winter during the snows, to run his trails one had to know the trees, ridges and swales individually to find the way because the drifts, the blow-downs and the laid-over branches utterly altered the landscape, erasing Gus' subtle signposts. Gus knew everything there was to know about these woods—perhaps an exaggeration—but he certainly could talk long and eloquently, not to mention with a self-proclaimed authority, about how the terrain—literally the oldest on the surface of the earth—had been formed. Being an avid reader, like I said before, he knew how icy glacial fingers had ripped these gullies in their geologic retreat, and what the water had done over eons to shape this land. He would ramble on about the process of succession—how marshes turn into woods in the forest; or was it the other way around?

Anyway . . . I would find him. But where to look? The first place was at his camps, of course. This was logical. Perhaps he was out at Barking Bear, but I would go to Workman's Comp first, though I knew he probably wasn't there. I wished I had offered to drive him to Florida—pronounced "Flaaruduh" hereabouts—and then none of this would have happened. I putted along on the Ski-doo, making a good two miles per hour, which was very nearly top speed on the aged clunker. At that rate I might arrive at Barking Bear in my lifetime, which my paranoia had once again started telling me would be decidedly short. Gus' life by contrast seemed long and eventful, especially now that it was suffused with the aura of the eternal.

I got off the snowmobile from time to time, shutting off the engine—always risky out in the woods as the engine could get temperamental—and listened. I had a flashlight and checked a few places where I thought it was likely someone would pass through looking for Gus. The thought of the cops searching nagged at me like a toothache. But I found no sign. I found some tracks, but these were my own from the night before during the wounded-wolf fiasco, and I didn't want to think about that.

During his heyday, Gus had four cabins scattered around a wide-ranging trapping territory in the western Upper Peninsula. Plus he had at least a half-dozen lean-tos where he could hole up if need be—say if he was caught in a storm or was about to be pinched by the game warden. My favorite camp used to stand in what was a national wilderness area in the former Sylvania Tract south of where I was and on the other side of U.S. 2. It was a long trip by canoe and over trail, and I loved to go to that camp when I was a kid because the place was so mysterious in the way it kind of blended into the surroundings. I remember that the first time I went there, I walked right past it. I was ahead of Gus and didn't notice when he went inside, and I found myself hollering to beat the devil for him. When he poked his head out the door, I was so shocked I almost screamed.

I suppose that introduction was why I always thought of the place as somewhere where goblins, or at least elves and trolls, might want to hang around. The door and walls were moss-covered; the roof, made of cedar shingles, looked more like a sod roof than anything, as it even had small evergreens growing out of it where pine seeds had gained a foothold in the humus and needles blown there. The cabin, made of cedar logs, was rated about a hundred notches below a one star hotel, complete with a dirt floor covered with porcupine and mouse droppings. Needless to say, the stench inside was nearly unbearable. All of Gus' places were sparsely furnished, but this one was especially so with its homemade stove, plank table, a couple of chairs cut from logs with a chainsaw and a wooden platform covered by a tick mattress, which I always pummeled a little before lying down to rid it of garter snakes, weasels and whatnot that nested inside. I remember dozens of traps hanging from wooden pegs driven into the cedar walls, hide stretchers, tin pots, antlers and old clothes. Gus never threw anything away, and it seemed like anything that anyone else discarded Gus would pick up and take to camp.

That place was so foul and so funky that someone could have strung a red velvet rope around it and sold tickets to tourists. It was a real wart, and since the goddamn Feds were anxious to keep Gus out of the area, they burned the place down. Or so Gus said, and I'm not sure how he knew who did it. Anyway, after feeling gloomy about it for a while, Gus shot out a tire on a government vehicle down by Robbin's Pond one night—his first sniper hunt, so to speak—causing the driver to swerve off the gravel road and into a ditch. The truck was a total loss, but Gus said it meant a lot less to the government than the cabin in the Sylvania had meant to him. I had to agree. I had shot my first deer there at Camp Waboose, which means rabbit in the Anishinabe language. The deer had only one antler though, which I discovered only on inspecting the kill close up, and so I was heartbroken, as I had wanted very badly to kill a "real" buck. Gus went ahead and sawed off the top of the deer's head, and the skull cap with the single antler attached to it went up on the wall with the rest of the so-called trophies. Gus said that my deer had lost his other antler in a fight, so that one remaining horn was proof that he had spirit. My unicorn, as I called it, burned up in the fire with everything else.

It had started to snow again. Was this to be a record winter? One learns to take this in stride in the U.P., and Finns are supposed to be so cold-blooded, but this winter seemed particularly heavy. I felt the wind come up and the temperature start to drop, so I stopped the snowmobile again and cinched the hood of my parka tighter around my face. I shut the engine off again and listened to the clacking of branches high up in the trees and the mournful moaning of deadfalls rubbing against the trunks of big popple. Then a tree went down somewhere to the east. A great crash echoed through the woods, and I, momentarily breathless, did not have a thought left in my brain. I flipped the half-smoked cigarette that had gone out and stuck to my lip into a snowbank and began pulling on the starter rope. On the seventh try the engine caught.

I started out and for some reason started thinking about Gus' camp over by the Lake of the Clouds, some thirty miles to the north below a ridge that ran along Lake Superior below the village of Ontonagon at the mouth of the river of the same name. This camp was a little nicer place than Waboose as far as comfort was concerned. It was really old, and Gus was always repairing it, so, oddly enough, it owned a finished quality that all the others, except the WPA shack, lacked. It was called Camp Dido, although I can only guess why. Dido was a nickname for Charlie hereabouts, and it may have been named for Charlie Salo whose arm Gus almost cut off with an axe one time.

What happened was that some men were dragging a big buck out of a cedar swamp down by that camp. They had to keep cutting brush and small trees to get the deer up the side of a steep ravine at its mouth, and as Gus swung the axe to take off a tree limb, Charlie lost his footing and his arm slipped between the axe and the branch. The blade cut right through the bone on Charlie's upper arm, leaving it attached only by a strip of muscle. Fortunately Gus was a whiz with first aid, having seen a lot of accidents like this in the woods, so he and the others saved Charlie. After surgery and a long period of rehabilitation, Charlie Salo was okay. And he never held it against Gus as far as I knew.

That incident occurred well before my time, as almost everything connected with this place was. Dido also meant a rip-roaring good time or whatever, and that was how I connect the place with the name. It was there that I cut my first "dido," getting drunk and passing out on the plank floor. I was just fourteen, and Gus was angry but only because I had drunk his emergency pint of Ever-Clear, a substance that I never touched again as it was too ferocious. Twenty-five years later my stomach still clenched with the thought of that particular morning after.

That was one of the few times I ever heard Gus curse too. Some people liked to call him Gus-the-Cuss, a name literally inappropriate because Gus was somewhat prissy and puritanical when it came to profanity, especially when kids, who tend to-wards overkill, swore. I could never use the F-word around him; that was where his generation drew the line, and, in turn, was beyond where his father's generation drew it. To my grandpa, swearing was as blasphemous as any black sin and was way up toward the top of a long list of things that could land a person in hell. I stopped the snowmobile again to savor a bitter memory that had remained buried for a long, long time.

When I was about ten years old, I went into Ewen with Gus in his old, doorless Plymouth that had a wasp's nest hanging from the rearview mirror right in the front seat. Gus wouldn't let any-one bother that nest as he said it discouraged auto thieves—not that anyone would even think of stealing that hunk of junk on wheels. Anyway, Ewen had a sort of movie theatre at that time; Gus dropped me there when he went to Connie's Tap to toss back a few with the boys. When the movie let out, Gus was still in the bar, and I had to wait several hours until it closed. When he came out, he was pretty blasted and wanted me to drive, which I had never done, except for the old Oliver tractor Grandpa owned. But I managed to get us out to the farm, and, since it was so late, I decided to sleep on one of the beds up-stairs opposite Gus' room instead of calling my father to come and get me. It must have been three in the morning when we came in. Gus sent me to bed after telling me that he was going to heat up some water on the stove to fix himself a hot toddy. Well, I could hear him whistling and clanking around down in the kitchen, and I could also hear my grandpa tossing in his bed and grumbling about the noise Gus was making. Pretty soon Gus stomped upstairs with a lantern in one hand, a Zane Grey novel tucked under his arm, and his cup of whiskey, honey and hot water in his other hand. He got undressed, tossed his heavy boots around and bounced on the squeaky springs, singing a ribald Finnish folksong in a loud voice. About the time he settled into the sack, I heard my grandpa bellow like an enraged bull and come pounding up the stairs. He stormed past my bed and burst into Gus' room. He snatched the lantern off the bedside table and then went back downstairs, leaving Gus in the dark. What happened then terrified me. Gus started screaming oaths at his father and then vowed to kill him. Swearing like the devil himself, he ran downstairs. I could hear him loading a rifle. Both of them—Gus and Grandpa—were yelling their heads off, and I was sure somebody was going to die. I wept and trembled as I listened to Gus let fly with a string of terrible curse words. I heard the old man cry out: "That's it, you no-good." And then silence as Gus left. Later Gus told me that the old man had meant what he said: That he now only had one son—my dad—and Gus was a stranger, welcome no more. They never spoke beyond what was absolutely necessary after that, and then never a kind or encouraging word. The old man had given up on his son. As in for good. A hard life for both of them—and hard felt by all.

A while later, in a mood of expectation occasioned by my thinking about Gus, I got to Workman's Comp and was almost surprised to find the place deserted. Other than me the night before, of course, no one had been there. Even Hairy Legs wasn't around. It seemed so lonely and forlorn that I didn't want to stay longer than necessary, deciding to make the trek to Barking Bear even though there was a chance that the cops would either be there or else would be watching for Gus along the way. Where in hell was he? And why this mysterious mumbo-jumbo about a gift and my having to find him?

Then it occurred to me that Dan and Eddie might have set this whole thing up, not Gus. He must have died, and they had put the body somewhere, wanting me to deal with it so they wouldn't have to contend with police questioning or whatever. Indians weren't treated very well by the cops around here—to say the least—so, if that were true, I couldn't really blame them for staying out of it. But, on the other hand, that didn't explain why they wouldn't tell me where he was in the first place. Nope. That wasn't it, I guessed. Cut it off twice, and it was still too short, as Gus might say.

I was having trouble with the snowmobile's headlight, which had a loose wire. I looked around in Gus' junk at Workman's Comp for some solder or something, but all I came up with was a roll of mouse-eaten electrical tape, which would probably work, although if it got any colder out, wouldn't stick. I sorted through Gus' stuff for a while. A strange taxonomy of items from a kind of fantastic junk menagerie: a piece of raw copper; a hand-carved pike plug with absurd eyes painted on the snout; some ball-bearings; a photo of Grandpa's mean dog, Gus holding its head in his lap; a broken, hand-carved board for stretching muskrat hides; a pair of collar stays; a whistle from a box of Cracker Jacks; assorted bolts, screws, hooks, nails, wire and buttons; a miniature oil can for servicing fishing reels; a couple of Hershey's Kisses; a blackened Mercury head dime; some bent washers used on beaver sets as drowning rings; a couple of hand-made tools—pullers or prys of some kind; a compass face—sans case, needle and liquid; another photo, of me feeding a bottle to the pet deer they kept on the farm for a few months. I found myself weeping at the sight of that deer, and I guessed at the boy who was just as long gone.

On the way out of the camp, I ran the snowmobile up on the snow-covered pyramid of whiskey bottles I should have remembered. I had stacked them there one day a long time earlier while I was stuck waiting for Gus to come back from checking his traps. This was when I was fourteen and had spent most of the winter on the farm or in the woods with Gus. Dad had grown sick of my sitting around the house eating and watching television, so I was sent out to the farm to work with Grandpa and learn some of the hard lessons of life. As I said, Grandpa was mean-spirited, so I avoided him as much as possible and took my lessons with Gus, which was by far better than going to school: I was absent almost a hundred days that year.

Gus allowed me to accompany him when he checked his trap lines. I would start off for school from the farm with only semi-honorable intentions anyway, and, to my delight, Gus would often intercept me on the road to town. Of course, I almost always knew when Gus was getting ready to go out into the woods because he'd put his Duluth pack on the back porch. Whenever I saw it there, the next morning I would put on my old clothes instead of my school clothes and sneak out without speaking to Grandpa or Grandma, both of whom looked like they were looking eternity in the face anyway and didn't pay much attention to the likes of an adolescent boy.

Gus' interpretation of the Code on the matter of travel in the woods was to travel light going out because you'd have a heavy load of furs or whatever coming back. I was along to serve as a pack mule, but it was a privilege for which a lot of the boys in high school would have traded their left nut because Gus was the first among equals in a whole region full of premier woodsmen, and to go trapping with him—especially poaching—was something special, a royal privilege. Whenever I wound up back in school, sometimes pinched by the truant officer and sometimes by Grandpa or my dad, I would spin wild yarns about Gus and me taking on wolf packs, crazed bears and trigger-happy game wardens.

As I thought about this, I wondered whether some of the lies I told contributed to Gus' troubles with the law, as kids told and retold those stories with fantastic embellishment. Among those who heard these tales were surely some who were not all that impressed or sympathetic and could have reported Gus to the authorities. I was sobered by the thought that I may have contributed to Gus' misery over the years. Too late to fix that one.

But didn't he get a lot of labor out of me? Like I said, I was just a pack mule, and Gus wouldn't let me near any of his sets; and if danger was near, I was the first to be hustled out of harm's way. So I didn't really see a lot in terms of crimes and misdemeanors—apart from the goods themselves—but what I experienced tended to become part of me.

Gus was always so particular about everything—compulsive, really—which was the way I was, I guess. His trap lines were sacred in a way; he believed that all sorts of things would jinx them, or at any rate disturb the animals and keep them out of his traps and snares. He boiled his traps, rubbed them with cedar and also took painstaking, meticulous care with his baits and scents. And he had this thing about profaning the woods, which was something about pop tabs and candy wrappers, not to mention snowmobiles.

But he was also full of nonsense, too. For instance, he claimed that I had an odor that upset beaver and fox. I couldn't smell it, though I checked myself out many a time. I thought later it was just a ruse to keep me from knowing too much about how and where he worked. He allowed no talking or wandering around when I was in the woods with him to take care of business, which was a way to control me because otherwise—recall that this was when I was just a kid—I was a real motormouth who could never stop talking long enough to catch my breath. I also liked to go crashing off into the woods on my own, which Gus scolded me for time and time again. He once said that if he taped my mouth shut and nailed my feet to the floor, my flapping arms would generate enough wind to blow the roof off the house.

I dragged the snowmobile out of the broken whiskey bottles, taking care not to step in the wrong place and cut a hole in a boot. Then I began pulling on the snowmobile's starter rope. After about twenty pulls, I was sweating like a cannon barrel in a pitched battle, but the machine popped to a start, belching a black cloud of smoke into my face and casting a fluttery beam of light up the trail. I took off for Barking Bear knowing that the chances of getting lost after all the snow, not to mention traveling at night, were pretty good. But I had to do it anyway. Compulsive.

With luck it would take about three hours or so to get there, maybe less. If I had one of those new snowmobiles, maybe I could get there in half an hour. But no thanks. A friend of mine had one, which he let me drive around on Lake Superior during an ice fishing expedition off of Little Girl's Point. I opened up the throttle and took the machine up to about seventy miles per hour. I hit a snow drift and went airborne for a few seconds.

Nothing bad happened, but I decided against buying one. Maybe it was best to keep my clunker of a Ski-doo and warped snow-shoes and remain pure. Right.

Where would I have found the money for such an item anyway? We—my parents and I, I mean—seldom bought luxuries, but we were considerably better off than my grandparents, or Gus, who only had money one time. That was when he was hired by the government. He had been particularly adept at dodging the law during that time, and the Feds, frustrated with his continuing depredations, hired him to supply the Smithsonian Institute in Washington with new specimens of woodland animals, the old ones apparently having become too moth-eaten and dusty to look life-like to the tourists taking in the exhibits. Gus was essentially given a license to poach, although now in the name of science. In addition to collecting animals for a price, he supplied biologists and other scientists of wildlife with data of various kinds. As a result of his virtual immunity from arrest, we ate high off the hog for several winters while the tree farming business was taking hold. In addition to the official market for the furs and such, the usual characters lined up to buy whatever surplus Gus had.

But I guess that business of selling to the government offended Gus' refined outlaw sensibilities, however, for he upgraded his drinking from a quart to two quarts of whiskey per day. His last trip for the government was the one when he dumped the canoe in the rapids and was saved by Eddie and Dan. I guess they were his real social workers, not Nora, because they sure did a job with him, while she had made me into a case.

The tape on the headlight wire froze and curled up, so I stopped to fix it. I was dizzy from the exhaust. It was positioned so that the driver always got a snoot full, and I took a rag and wiped away the carbon from my face. Riding that Ski-doo long enough made one start to resemble a raccoon. The engine died again, and I cussed it long and loud. Obviously I was going to have to replace it with the engine from a second snowmobile that I owned, which I had purchased for spare parts. I had bought it off an old badger who had gone to Florida a few years back, his circulatory system too crudded up from a lifetime of eating bakery, head cheese and half-and-half—not to mention from working in White Pine mine and breathing mining fumes—to be able to handle the U.P.'s winters any longer. This time I must have pulled that damned starter rope three dozen times before the engine caught—a good way to keep warm but decidedly hard on the old system.

Off again, paying attention now because no trail existed and the moon had disappeared, leaving the landscape as dark as the inside of a cow. It was cold, and I was exhausted by the time I reached Barking Bear. I was hopeful, but no Gus. I built a fire in the stove and scrounged around until I found an unlabeled can that turned out to be beef stew. I heated it and ladled its greasy contents out with a big spoon. I had lost my water bottle along the way, but there was a little filmy water in a blue plastic jug with a rusty cap. It didn't smell very good, but I drank some anyway, mostly to keep myself from getting dehydrated, if I wasn't already. I started to think about Nora and the warrant and Gus being dead, but managed to get into some serious kindling chopping to keep my mind from going maudlin. As I was chopping, I was certain that I heard the wolf again, but whatever had howled stopped as soon as I lay the hatchet down.

I was always hearing things in the woods—until I listened for them, of course. The woods to me were full of mystery—sounds with unknown sources, fleeting shapes and forms that disappeared on investigation, places that evoked special feelings, sensations and moods. As far back as I could remember, I had always been afraid of the woods, even after I came back to the farm from college. There were frightening places that I wouldn't visit, which made my dread of being alone all the more palpable—an odd situation for an old boar like me. But small triumphs also came in the form of discoveries that I made about the woods, and hence about myself. Gus had always told me to observe, to pay attention to what I was doing and to what the woods and the woodland animals were doing. As much as he liked to dramatize his exploits and exaggerate the danger, ad-

venture and struggle involved in living off the land, he never-
theless remained pretty much in control. Or a lot more than me,
at any rate.

One spring day when I was a kid, I was out at the farm visiting my grandparents. Standing in the yard, I heard what I
thought was a pump. The sound seemed to be coming from the
direction of Workman's Comp, so I went to see what Gus might
be up to. But he wasn't there, and I started back. Pretty soon I
heard the sound again, only it came from a different direction—
perhaps down by the river—so I turned to try to locate it. On
reaching the river I hadn't found anything, so I started back for
the farmhouse. The woods were intensely green—large, trembling popple and red pines with new growth and newly leaved-
out hickory and unfolding ferns. Plus bears had left plenty of
signs that they had been after insects in the ancient, weathered
pine stumps. The stumps had been torn asunder and their roots
dug out and scattered around the meadow, giving it the look of
a war zone. I got a little nervous on seeing these stumps and decided to trot back to the house. And as the picture of bears ripping stumps open grew more vivid in my mind with each step I
took, I was soon running in terror, lest I let my imagination carry
me into a bear's ferocious, slobbery maw. Crossing a narrow,
grassy corridor between rows of evergreens, I tripped over an
exposed root of a bush and fell head-long into a grove of sapling
spruce.

Lying there breathless for a moment, I again heard the
pum-pum-pum-pum-pum of that mysterious machine or whatever the hell it was. But this time it was quite close—in fact,
just ahead of me. Staying low, I cautiously moved some branches
aside just in time to see a male grouse strutting along a fallen,
moss-covered log. He clutched the moss with his feet and began
drumming with his wings. Pum-pum-pum-pum-pu-pu-pu-pah.
He did it several times, and several nearby females watched
him attentively. I got up after a while and walked proud as punch
back to the farm.

After that incident I was more convinced that whatever I
encountered in the woods wouldn't be too bad, provided I

watched my step and didn't come between a sow black bear and her cubs or sit under a tree in a lightning or windstorm. Much of my fear of nature was drummed out of me that day, though the woods still owned an ominous flavor.

But I had to deal with other fears. Especially when I discovered, after Mom's death and Dad's suicide, that I was alone and that I, too, would someday die. What was life about? Were we all like Christmas trees—born to be cut down? Decorated, celebrated, then thrown out? It wasn't a comforting thought. What was Gus trying to prove? Or for that matter, what about me? The big macho. Never showing emotion, always forcing down the feelings that threatened to rise with the tides of experience. And how Nora had laid that delusion to rest.

I lingered there in Barking Bear hoping Gus would come back but knowing that he wouldn't. How could he if he was dead? I sat on a broken chair, my feet up on the table, thinking. Suddenly I realized that I might have had a different life if I had allowed myself to, and if I had expected more of myself. How did it happen that little by little I had come to believe that my own life wasn't worth all the bother it would take to make it into something, or even to satisfactorily explain it to myself, for that matter? I also had the sensation of having to justify something. What was I required to justify? My feelings about Gus? Certainly. I loved that old buck. Or maybe it was love/hate. These feelings would take a long time to sort out. And what about Nora? That might take even longer. I had deliberately conditioned myself to think of my life as unworthy of a full-time course of study. The folly of an unexamined life was probably overrated anyway. I knew plenty of only moderately miserable people who would have been a lot unhappier had they spent more time in contemplation of the causes of their suffering. At least they knew what to expect and didn't delude themselves with false hopes about achieving happiness. Of course, this made them a bit oblique, but then why should people be on display like TV stars or window mannequins, even if only to themselves? Did ravens think like this? It was the agitated, cultured mind that labeled our unhappiness and thus provided the draft to enflame

103

our perpetual disequilibrium. People were just plain over-stimulated. Me, I have a tree farm to keep me focused. Had a tree farm. Now I had Nora. And Gus, if I could find him.

And Gus had me. He had never had anyone else. He had always been alone, despite friends, relatives, poaching and drinking buddies. People were always angry with him or nervous around him. His parents . . . well, that was just sad. My dad, his brother . . . another case in point illustrating Gus' estrangement. He never married, of course, and he often said that I should watch out because I might wind up like him. "These woods will become your life, and then you'll see, Harry."

What I was supposed to see, I hadn't the foggiest idea.

8

Echoes of Gus: "What a knobhead you are, Harry," Nora said in response to my whining inquiry about why she had gone to Marquette—as if she had to check with me first; as if her absence had caused me to go through the wringer; as if she was obligated to hang around and help me. As soon as the words left my mouth, I wanted to call them back because I could see that she was really disappointed in me. I hadn't meant to sound so . . . well . . . what was the word? Dependent? Demanding? Certainly. Add manipulative. It was an uncomfortable moment that gave birth to something that, I realized, would make things harder for us to carry on our relationship simply because it wouldn't by itself pass away and would require some delicate negotiations and self-revealing honesty. Yes, some sort of knobhead.

What had happened? I had declared myself to be four-square for the tradition wherein the woman answered to the man. I tried to rationalize that I was not used to independent women—that I wasn't all that experienced with the new rules.

But at the same time I couldn't really imagine myself in a relationship with a traditional woman, one who knew her place and kept her own counsel, who never had a self of her own, or a life.

In the past, couples were dependent on one another, the man and woman being fixed in complementary, albeit sometimes overlapping, roles. The men plowed, and the women cooked. The men cut wood, and the women maintained the house. But both harvested the crops, tended the gardens and carried water. If one didn't fulfill the other's expectations, the whole thing fell apart because the contribution of each was the condition for the continuity of the whole.

My grandmother seldom had left the farm, and when the farm failed, she went down with it. Grandma died within weeks of Grandpa, as if a common lifeline sustained them, and when it was broken by his death, her own end was inevitable. My mother and my father were molded in a similar pattern. They both tended the variety store, but Dad dealt with the bank and with the wholesalers while Mom kept the books and the stock. Even after the store burned, they quickly re-established that continuity of their lives out on the farm. But then Mom died, and Dad was adrift. He floated for a while but couldn't maintain his internal buoyancy.

Now with Nora and me—the same thing, only it wouldn't work in the same way. We were both independent. Why should she give independence up for me; why should I want her to? I didn't really want a "wife" in the old sense, and I was sure she didn't want a mere husband. But how did we form a union with two independent persons without one or the other of us giving up the autonomy and independent spirit that had formed the basis of the attraction in the first place? It wasn't simply a case of reciprocal sacrifice, of tit for tat. Wasn't this the way things always happened in relationships: A nightmarish, slow-motion descent that couldn't be diverted or stopped? I knew I was blowing it, and badly, with Nora. How could I keep myself from acting the fool, when there was no precedent for acting otherwise?

"Nora, I'm sorry," I said, taking her by the hand. "It's just that. . . ." And I told her about the wolf, about coming back and finding Eddie and Dan in the sauna, and what they had said about Gus having died, and finally about circling around in the woods all night on the snowmobile trying to find him but without the slightest clue as to where to look. I was changing—that's what all this seemed to suggest. Fair enough. And my need to include her in my life was real. So what is your problem, Harry? "Get with the 'po-gram,'" as Gus would say.

Nora asked me if I had checked all of Gus' secret places in the woods—not only the camps, but his deer blinds and lean-tos—and she told me to try again to think about what he might do. Or what I might do under the circumstances. But I just couldn't think. The bubble had burst. And so soon! I finally just gave up: "What's going on? I know I'm blowing it with you; but I try to . . . you and me . . . I mean, are we together or what?"

"Yes," she said, "but we have to work things out; it'll take time is all, and I think you have to work on yourself a little, Harry." We were in the kitchen, and she hadn't even taken off her coat. Now she stood up and went to the door, stopping with her hand on the doorknob. "And as far as Gus is concerned, and the gift, I think this is something you have to deal with," she said, opening the door.

I stood up and faced her. She looked at me, and I felt a vast expanse of space opening up and separating us. I put a hand on her shoulder and then touched her hair. She moved her head to one side and a frown creased her forehead. I leaned over to kiss her, and she turned a cheek to me.

"Okay" I said, "I'll do my best. I really care for you, Nora."

"I know. And I care for you, too."

She let me give her a brief hug, and then she turned and went out. I watched her from the porch as she drove up the driveway in the Bronco. I knew I was blowing it. Had she lived independently for so long only to fall into my orbit? Only a fool would think so. I stared dumbly at the driveway for a long time, and it was a few seconds before the car registered in my mind. A police car, of course. Tony Coelho and Norb.

Damn, not now, I thought. I watched them come to the door and knock—a loud, insistent pounding. I let them in.

Tony got right to the point. "Okay, Harry, let's have it."

"Have what?" I smiled sheepishly at him, wishing I had a lot more self-control and realizing at the same time that I was in deep shit. He never acted like this, not even when he had toyed with the idea that I might have done Gus in.

"Cut the crap. Where's Gus?" Tony was all cop now. His detached, self-effacing style was nowhere in evidence. I was strictly a suspect or an impediment to an investigation or something.

"I . . . he's . . . ah . . . ." I stopped. Should I tell him? I didn't want to involve Eddie and Dan, although I simultaneously realized that they could probably handle the sheriff better than I could, Indians in the U.P. being a customary, perpetual focus of official action, and thus pretty experienced.

Norb was expressionless as usual, but Tony seemed impatient, angry even. "He's what?" Tony insisted.

"Dead," I said.

"Dead . . . mm-hmm." Tony didn't believe me.

"Then where's the body?" Norb asked. Tony glared at him fiercely, and Norb looked down, embarrassed at having butted in.

"Answer the question," said Tony.

"Really, I don't know," I replied. "He, he . . . ah. . . ."

"You have about two seconds, Harry, before we take you to Ontonagon and book you for obstructing an investigation, and I'm sure we can add a few more charges to keep you around for a while. You don't want that to happen do you?" He smiled patronizingly.

"No, but I don't see why you. . . ."

"The straight story, Harry. Norb . . ." Tony nodded to Norb who slowly removed a set of handcuffs from the case on his belt and held them up in front of my face.

I stared at them. "Ah . . . you're not really going to. . . ."

"Go ahead, Norb," said Tony.

In about the time it takes to swallow one's tongue, my hands were behind my back. I was surprised at how deftly Norb—who was about as dainty as a moose—slapped on the steel bracelets.

They pinched my wrists, and I felt my shoulder in Norb's grip. He pushed me through the kitchen door, then hauled me across the porch, down the steps, and shoved me into the back seat of the squad car—all in about five seconds.

Tony took his time getting behind the wheel. He put an arm up on the seat and spoke to me through a little opening in the plexiglass that separated the front seat from the back. "Harry, this is it."

"I don't know where he is. All I know is that he's dead." I was too upset now to tell him anything more—even if I wanted to. Plus my hands hurt, and I couldn't find a comfortable position on the car seat.

"How do you know he's dead?"

"Two friends of his . . . they came out here and told me." I could feel my hands going numb, but my wrists still burned from the handcuffs. "Jesus Christ, Tony, loosen these cuffs, will you? I'll tell you everything I know."

"Quit fighting them. Relax. Which friends of Gus'?"

"I don't know them," I said.

"You don't know them?" He snorted. "Jesse Maki?"

"No, Jess is in Arizona. I told you I don't know them."

"Emil Daagsgard?"

"No! Emil still drinks and Gus doesn't. . . ."

"Who then? Somebody from Bruce Crossing, Watersmeet. . . ."

"No. Tony, loosen the cuffs, my hands are going to fall off," I pleaded.

God, what was with this guy? I couldn't believe it. I was going to jail. What if they found the wolf? Did they know that I had put Gus' coat in the beaver pond and sent them on a wild goose chase? Nora certainly wouldn't have told them, but maybe they had figured it out for themselves.

"Are these guys Indians? Seems to me he was hanging around. . . ." Tony stopped in mid-sentence and studied my face. I must have given off some sort of sign because he grinned and then picked up the radio and called the dispatcher. "Adele, this is Tony. I got Harry, and we'll be bringing him in. Pull Gus' file and see what it says about those Indian guys he was hanging around with. Get back to me. Ten-four."

He turned the car around in the drive, and then we sat there for a few minutes with the engine idling. I was sweating bullets though I didn't have my coat, and the heater was off. Norb stared at me the whole time, and I went through a gamut of emotions from fear to outrage and finally calm. I tried to stop myself, but I couldn't help but laugh. Tony cut his eyes at me and lit a cigar. Norb was impassive. What a tree!

The radio squawked, and Tony listened as the disembodied voice read him a few lines from Gus' file. I heard the names Eddie Small Legs and Dan Foucault. I was amazed at what the cops knew about Gus' private life. From what I gathered a couple of months earlier, in the late summer or early fall, the police had stopped to check out why they were parked alongside the road. Gus had gotten ornery, but the two Indians had cooled the situation out. Eddie was given a ticket for numerous safety violations and had never had them cleared.

"Is there a warrant on that?" Tony asked.

"Not yet," I heard Adele say. "You bringing Harry in?"

"Affirmative," said Tony coldly. He glanced back at me, a dispassionate, telling look.

During the drive to Ontonagon and the county jail, I felt very detached, but at the same time things had an almost super-real quality to them. The snow that covered everything had a bluish cast, reflecting the cloudless sky. Everything looked peaceful around Ewen—a few skiers driving to Indianhead and Powderhorn in the Gogebic Range over by Ironwood; a couple of men scraping snow off the ice-skating pond near the edge of town, and a group of kids, their skates already on, standing at the ready; a knot of people bent over a broken-down snowmobile with its hood raised; cars in line at the Co-op gas pumps; an old man carrying his dog up a driveway; old farm machinery barely visible beneath the snow; more snowmobilers working on their machines, with other helmeted, space-suited members of the party pacing around; and, finally, a long, flying caravan of ravens traveling at tree-top level up the South Branch of the Ontonagon River, which, when we crossed the bridge, looked like a melted stream of butterscotch filled with puffy, white marshmallows.

Sitting in the moving cage. No door handles or window cranks. Grey plastic seat covers. Was I under arrest? There had been no formal statement to that effect. Why hadn't I been read my rights? I did have some, didn't I, this being America and all? Even if it was the U.P. and even if they did things a little differently here.

But like I said, I was perfectly calm. In fact, I was thinking about how to repair the rift with Nora, which had begun over such a stupid thing and then became a widening gyre. I would show her I was capable of a mature relationship. And then I thought about how to go about finding Gus. Or should I find Gus first? I stopped myself just short of the thought that if I were in jail, I would at least be able to figure out what to do—and how to do it. But no, I was not going to get comfortable with the idea of steel and concrete. Instead, I tried to think of how I could get Tony to release me without giving him any information. Besides, didn't he have the information he needed already? His hauling me in was just a show of police power. "It is not good to put the cops in that position, Harry." Gus had told me that.

A half-hour later we pulled up to a yellowish brick structure and took a plowed, snowbank-lined circular drive around the back where they brought in prisoners. To my surprise and relief, Nora's Bronco was parked there. Adele and Nora were friends, and Adele must have called her. Norb told me to get out and hustled me inside the building. Tony rushed off somewhere, and, before he came back, I could hear him yelling and arguing with Nora and a third person. When Tony came back to the booking desk, he told Norb to put me in a room nearby, where I sat on a folding chair. I was there long enough to fight down a panic attack, and then Tony came in with Buzz Tarantino, a lawyer, and removed the handcuffs. My hands were painfully swollen. Buzz looked them over with his lawyer's eyes. He shook his head and looked accusingly at Tony, who by this time was back in his "Ah, shucks" mode.

"Harry," said Buzz, "Nora told me you were being arrested, but I guess that isn't the case, right Tony?"

Buzz was a tall, lean guy who weighed about as much as a
great blue heron; he would float away in a strong wind. He always wore a suit—a most unusual uniform around these parts—
and had a reputation as an obstinate sort, though his manner
was casual enough, and he always got along with everybody.
Usually he acted as Public Defender and was full of legal tricks,
which sometimes caused people to think that he might be a lib-
eral, a stigma one didn't relish if expecting to be a part of the
community. But Buzz was pretty generous and civic-minded and
had helped me out with the estate when Dad died. He had not
even charged an arm and a leg for his services, which he had
performed with apparent competence. I didn't really know him
that well, but I knew Nora had probably picked him to represent
me because he would make the cops stick to the rules.

Tony explained that he was under a lot of pressure from the
Feds and the DNR to do something about Gus, and then, after
apologizing to me, he cut me loose under the condition that I
wouldn't leave the county. Nora was waiting outside when I
walked out of the building. I got into the Bronco and didn't say
anything, still somewhat stunned at the rapidity of events—not
to mention their apparent randomness.

"Hi," she finally said.

"Hi," I answered.

"You okay?" She touched my swollen hand.

I looked at my hands and rubbed them together. "Yeah, I
think so. A close call, wouldn't you say? Thanks, Nora."

She nodded. "You want to come over to my place? Maybe
we should talk."

"Uh . . . I have to. . . ."

"Your place then?"

I nodded. We drove in silence to the farm. I got out, and she
told me to call her when I wanted to talk, as it was obvious that
I was in no shape to do so then.

"I'm sorry," I said.

She nodded, and I shut the door and went inside as she drove
away. I relit the kitchen stove and put some water on to boil. As
I sat looking out the window at the chickadee pecking away at

the string bag of suet hanging from the feeder, I was pole-axed by a sudden, profound revelation: I knew what had happened to Gus. And where to find him. Wasn't it obvious?

I got up, turned off the water, banked the fire and put on my cap, parka, mittens and boots. I grabbed the snowshoes off the back porch, buckled them on and headed east toward the river. Crossing the little meadow where the old washing machine stood, I went up to it and looked inside. The rifle I had put there was gone, as I expected it would be. The machine had belonged to us, and when Dad bought Mom a new one, my folks had given it to my grandparents. Dad had always been after Grandpa to put running water in the house, but the old man had refused. Eventually Gus had hauled the thing out to the meadow where it became a kind of storage bin for whatever he didn't want in the house. Being right out in the open like that, he figured no one would ever think to look in it. As far as I knew, he was right, too.

I replaced the lid and continued on toward the river, checking a few spots where Gus snared grouse under pine bough shelters. Well in advance of my arrival at the river, which was a little over a mile from the house, I could hear the ravens, and, as I got to the river bank, I could see them. There were hundreds of them in the big trees that lined both sides of the flood channels of an old ox-bow. Gus had often used this place to hunt deer. Often, when we'd see a deer flashing through the woods, we'd run down there and wait. Invariably the deer would show up and Gus would make the kill. He had a big blind made of bolts of popple and cedar that braced a platform of rough-sawn pine. Well camouflaged, the pine stained and darkened, it was maybe thirty feet off the ground high up in a tight cluster of mature pines. It was invisible from the ground because of the position of the lower tree branches, and invisible from the air because of the tops of the trees, plus some touches Gus had added with chicken wire and cut boughs.

As I approached the spot, I could see the ravens jammed shoulder to shoulder on the platform. Two ropes hung down the trunk of one massive tree, the block and tackle just below a thick branch that served as one support for the platform. I stared up into the tree tops for a few moments, listening to the ravens, whose calling had become more excited due to my presence. At the base of the tree, there were tracks in the snow, evidence that someone had recently been there. And not one, but two sets of tracks. The cops? Tourists? No, it had to have been Eddie and Dan.

Don't ask me how I did it, but I managed to get up that tree using the block and tackle. The ravens took off in an explosive black cloud and rose high above the trees circling and swooping and calling to one another before organizing themselves into flights that left one wave at a time for the south and the thick, dark forests where they could find another undisturbed place to carry on their national affairs.

The platform was rickety, and I had to deal with vertigo for a few moments. The loose pine needles formed a thick bed, and the place smelled from the raven droppings and, of course, what they had been feeding on. There wasn't much left of Gus, or the wolf either for that matter. A porcupine had pretty much taken care of the rifle stock, and the scope and barrel were already rusty. Gus' home-made skinning knife with its taped handle was still attached to his belt, so I took it off—carefully, so as not to disturb the bones even though scattered and twisted like they were, they didn't much resemble a skeleton—and then covered everything with pine needles. Little pieces of cloth—Gus' shirt and pants—were scattered around everywhere, but his hat was more or less intact so I put it in my pocket. I unhooked the block and tackle, dropping it to the ground.

While climbing down—sliding first from one branch to the other on the sappy, flaking trunk—I recalled the time I was fourteen and the game warden had closed in on Gus. He was about to go down for the count, but he wasn't going to let those furs go either. On that occasion it was a bale of bobcat, fox, beaver, marten, and, as I recalled, a big wolverine. It weighed about as much as a wheelbarrow full of clay, and Gus filled another pack with chunks of hard maple and put it on my back. He then slung his topcoat over my shoulders and plopped his WW-I campaign hat on my head, cinching the leather chin strap tight. After he dropped me off with his old Hudson, I put on the snowshoes and walked down to the river off Cemetery Road, letting the game warden who was waiting there to intercept Gus see me cross at one of his known fording places. In the meantime, Gus doubled back and sold the fur to a buyer waiting on the other side of Ewen. When the game warden finally caught up with me, needless to say he was surprised I wasn't Gus. He was really pissed off to find that pack of firewood too. Nor could I explain what I was up to. Not that I had to: The game warden knew only too well. He took me back to the farm, and both he and my grandfather yelled at me for quite a while.

Secretly I felt great, although I wept and begged for mercy. Later on, though, I felt used when I found out that Gus had gone on the lam in Canada. Every day, Grandpa warned me against becoming a worthless, drunken violator like Gus, and after a while I started thinking that the old man was right. I was well on my way to reforming, vowing to myself to stay away from Gus and perhaps even turn him in sometimes if I felt the urge. But then a couple of months later Gus showed up and gave me a new rifle that he had bought with the money from the furs, thus ending any further thoughts on my part of betraying him, or of becoming a solid citizen for that matter.

I didn't feel like going back to the farm just then, so I set out instead on a long trek across country to Barking Bear. I arrived just before dark, having made good time along the ridges that criss-crossed the woods. I lit a fire in the stove, messing with the flue for quite a while before I got it going. When it finally caught, I closed the damper, and the cabin heated right up. It soon got so hot I had to start peeling off my clothes. Gus' bad heart had made his circulation poor, so he always kept the fire too hot, which I could never get used to. Gus was just cold blooded, I guess, a condition I had had to get used to. Which was what always happened. You had to put up with others. How much was reasonable to impose on them? What was I trying to impose on Nora?

I propped open a window, finally, and left the door ajar. The draft made the yellow flame in the oil lamp flicker a little, and the close interior of the cabin pulsed and vibrated. Until my eyes adjusted, I had a sensation of vertigo. I found a gruesome head cheese and the inevitable jar of fecal-looking prunes. As I ate, I remembered that Gus had kept an emergency bottle of Ever-Clear under a loose floorboard in the corner. I retrieved it and poured myself an extra large shot of the stuff. I welcomed the almost instantaneous, stoned feeling I got, which was preferable to my previous lighter-than-air, almost floaty, state of mind.

I sat in camp staring at the antlers on the walls; the old traps rusting from disuse; the battered pots and skillet; the almost cavern-like quality of the cabin's interior, with its scarred log walls, loosely chinked with sphagnum moss and oakum, and the ceiling of rough-sawn popple, low and knotty with cobweb draperies; and the floors covered with assorted junk, magazines, empty cans and bottles, boxes of paperback books, a can of Neet's Foot Oil, and an old Winchester calendar from 1969, the year I hung out with Gus and nearly flunked out of school, but got an "A" from Gus.

I wished that I had said a proper good-bye to him, but then he wasn't much of a sentimentalist. How strange the sight of that wolf's skull next to his, and his arm, covered with shards of flesh and cloth, wrapped around the rib cage of the animal he had almost single-handedly brought to the brink of extinction in the U.P. Of course I had stupidly killed this animal. No need to blame Gus. Had I killed Gus, too? Nothing ironic here at all, I thought, which was always the trouble with Gus. To him normalcy was just a pin-hole in the fabric of unreality. He was gone, and, in a natural way, it was right that he should be. As for me. . . .

For all the official senior citizenry inflicted upon the U.P., people don't like the old-timers or those of us who still hold them up to be something special. Their skills seem obsolete. Cooking, building, making things, and, yes, living on the land—these things seem "other." Plus the fact that guys like Gus—what few of them there are around anymore—give the north country a bad name. They are in the way of progress and, therefore, an embarrassment. I think this is because we can see on their faces

that they know what we were up to, what all this tourist business
and community service shit really means. What it meant was that
the person didn't ski, the skis skied the person. People didn't
drive the snowmobile, it drove them. They didn't fish and hunt,
they shopped for fish and game. They didn't camp, the campsite
did it for them. The trail took them, they didn't take it. And all
of it made us into snapshots, the continuity of which was sustained by information which fit only with itself, not the place or
its history. Life became an "attraction": the Toonerville Trolly,
the World's Tallest Indian, the mining interpretative center, the
curio shop. The ecology and way of life of the U.P. were reduced
to fish tanks and maps and tape recorded messages. People
flashed on by, motors running.

The Ever-Clear reminded me of my exhaustion. The walls
of the cabin became oppressive. No thoughts of Nora now. I sat
idly scratching my ribs and remembered again the mystical year
of Gus' and my joint maneuvers in the woods, particularly what
had been its crowning moment, so to speak.

We were sitting at the table of Workman's Comp Camp. Gus
was so tanked that he would have blown up like the Hindenburg
if I had touched a match to him. He took off his frayed, mouse-
bit campaign hat and told me to look at his scalp right on the
crown of his skull. His hair was a weird, almost bottled color of
shoe-polish brown, thin and tamed with Wildroot Creme Oil.

"Do you see it?" he asked.

I studied his head. I thought I was looking for a tick or a
wound or something. Finally I told him there was nothing there
that I could see.

"Nothing there?" he roared, acting as though I were being
deliberately useless.

"What am I supposed to see?" I whined.

"The X," he yelled, "the X on my fucking head!" It was about
the only time I heard him use the F-word, which scared and
depressed me, for I was certain that it was not Gus but me who
carried the X meant by God to mark the one whose life was des-
tined to be especially screwed up.

I let the fire burn out and then started for the Fair Oaks

Road. When I got there I found Nora asleep in the Bronco, and I knocked on the window. She smiled and I got in. "Hello," I said, pleased that she had guessed that I would go to Barking Bear.

We kissed, and I held her for a long time.

"You found him," she said.

"Yes."

"And the gift."

"Yes."

"I'm glad," she said and started the engine.

For the rest of the winter, I took daily walks out to the beaver pond and imagined Gus living in the lodge with the beavers. He had grown a slick coat of mahogany-colored fur which he kept well oiled. His tail was broad and flat and made a resounding pop when he slapped it on the surface of the water to warn the others of danger—or, as was sometimes his wont, just for the hell of it. Nora often came with me and would let me carry on my dialogue with him. We visited the trees down by the river, too, but we never climbed up to the platform. Eventually, Nora stopped going with me, letting me keep the place to myself. Whenever I returned, she would ask me how he was doing. My answer was always, "The beavers say okay," or "The ravens say okay."

There wasn't much else to say, really. Whenever I thought about what Gus had done, I had to conclude that it was all right. I suppose he was returning the gift the forest had given him—his body in return for having been given sustenance and life. And of course there was the gift he gave to me and Nora—each other. What did I have to worry about now? Nothing. Everybody turned out to be pretty hopeful that Gus had escaped to Florida, and so his legend lived on. Tony Coelho had a close call with a challenger who tried to use the Gus incident to his own advantage, but Tony didn't let that bother him, and people accepted that he had mistreated me out of pressure from outsiders—which is still a good way to claim innocence. Nora and I moved in together in March, she coming out to the farm after putting her cabin up for sale. It wasn't as easy as we thought, because both of us had been used to bachelor living, but what is life if not adjustments? We got along okay. Pretty well in fact.

Epilogue

It was the day before the vernal equinox. A bright and clear day. Still late spring in that cold, tough country. Though another frost wouldn't come until the fall, in all probability, one had to be a little daring to put a garden in just yet, as the ground was still cold. Nora and Harry had some tomatoes in a cold frame. Like many others they were waiting until warmer weather. The leaves were small on the trees, and plenty of signs of the heavy snows of the past record winter existed; it had produced the most precipitation in memory. Grey, red and brown leaves were tamped flat with grasses and ferns just beginning to grow up underneath. The earth still exhaled a coolish breath, but clearly summer was coming. Mosquitoes buzzed listlessly, not yet lusting for blood. The primeval atmosphere of the grove of trees by the river seemed to penetrate the skin.

The couple spread a checkered cloth beneath the giant red pine. He opened a screw-top bottle of California zinfandel, and she took their lunch out of the pack. They ate cold rabbit and for dessert some bars that she baked that morning. They were chocolate, his favorite, though he didn't often eat them—only on special occasions—because he had taken to watching his weight and his cholesterol. They sat close to one another, almost touching, thoughtfully discussing the site, one of their favorite places to picnic (the other being in the little meadow next to the old washing machine). They felt like staying but decided to leave in case someone came along and spoiled the ambience of the setting and their special mood. At that time of year, backpackers were almost as thick as the mosquitoes in the woods. After they put away the wine bottle, the remains of the food, and folded up the table cloth, they spent a few minutes on their hands and knees looking for the tiny pieces of bone they sometimes found buried among the layers of pine needles. She found one, and they were delighted as they examined it closely. It would go into the old washing machine with the others they had collected. As they prepared to leave, they lifted their faces to the canopy above. The sunlight streamed through and reminded them of a cathedral. A group of ravens watched them from the platform high up in the trees. For a brief moment in those vast and wounded woods there was only the silence.

Jeremy Oswald

Joseph Damrell was born in Michigan and raised in Colorado and California. He moved to the Upper Peninsula in 1978 and spends as much time there as possible. He teaches at Northland College in Ashland, Wisconsin.

Other Finnish Titles by North Star Press

The Finn in Me: The Chronicles of a Karelian Emigrant
Sinikka Garcia

In Two Cultures: The Stories of Second Generation
Finnish-Americans
Edited by Aili Jarvenpa

A Field Guide to Blueberries
Jim Johnson

Isaac Polvi: The Autobiography of a Finnish Immigrant
Edited by Joseph Damrell

Karelia: A Finnish-American Couple in Stalin's Russia
1934-1941
*Lawrence and Sylvi Hokkanen
with Anita Middleton*

Helmi Mavis: A Finnish-American Girlhood
Mavis Biesanz

Finns in Minnesota Midwinter
James A. Johnson

Tuohela
Aili Jarvenpa

Half Immersed
Aili Jarvenpa